Night of Fire, Days of Rain

BOB ZOLLER

Regal
Books

A Division of GL Publications
Ventura, CA U.S.A.

Dedication:

To my wife Jan,
   for her patience,
     understanding,
      love and support.
But especially to our Lord,
   who has made all things possible.

The foreign language publishing of all Regal books is under the direction of GLINT. GLINT provides financial and technical help for the adaptation, translation and publishing of books for millions of people worldwide. For information regarding translation, contact: GLINT, P.O. Box 6688, Ventura, California 93006.

Published by Regal Books
A Division of GL Publications
Ventura, California 93006
Printed in U.S.A.

Library of Congress Cataloging in Publication Data

Zoller, Bob, 1948-
  Night of fire, days of rain.

  Summary: A mysterious stranger with a badly scarred face moves into a small town, where people are frightened of him at first but soon come to love him for his kindness.
  [1. City and town life—Fiction. 2. Christian life—Fiction] I. Title.
PZ7.Z73Ni   [Fic]   82-7491
ISBN 0-8307-0844-8   AACR2

Chapter One

He moved to a house just outside of town. Nobody even knew he was there before I saw him.

That was the scariest thing that had ever happened to me up till then. I'll never forget it, even though I was just a young schoolboy—more than 80 years ago. The year was 1898.

"Michael Roberts, you'd better get up," my mother called from the kitchen, "or you'll be late for school. This is an important day."

When she called me Michael Roberts I knew she meant business. Why was today so important? Oh, yes. The big geography test. Miss Hartfield expected us to know all 45 states of the United States.

I had been studying for weeks. Mother and Dad helped me as we sat by the fireplace in the evenings. They even had to learn some of the newer states—North and South Dakota, Montana, Washington, Idaho, Wyoming, and Utah. When they had studied the states in school there were only 38. The state of Colorado became the thirty-eighth state when our country was 100 years old.

As I stretched out under the warm blankets I heard Dad's boots clomp, clomp, clomping across the wooden floor. He opened the door to my room, and light from the kitchen jumped against the wall. Dad's huge shadow stood over me and his big voice prodded, "Michael, get up. Remember the deal we made!"

The deal was that I had agreed to do extra chores around the house if they helped me study the states. So, before I went to school I had to bring in some firewood, fill the lamps with kerosene and feed the chickens.

I pulled back the warm blankets and the thick down comforter and sat on the edge of the bed trying to wake up. It was always hard for me to wake up, but Mondays were the worst. My eyes felt like they had rocks in them. It was all I could do to force them open. My feet and legs dangled over the edge of the high bed and I shivered in the crisp October air. It was so cold I could see my breath. And the window glass was dripping wet with melting frost.

I pulled on my Levis over my long johns and tiptoed over to the washstand. The cold air blew up through the cracks between the floorboards. The small throw rug in front of the washstand felt good under my bare feet. I poured water out of the big white pitcher into the big white washbowl. Just the thought of washing with that cold water gave me goose bumps. I washed as fast as I could, with as little water as possible.

I quickly ran the brush through my dark brown hair. I stared into the cracked mirror at my freckled face. I hated those freckles, but Mother said they would disappear when I got older. The piece of paper stuck in the frame of the mirror said, "This is the day which the Lord hath made; we will rejoice and be glad in it," Psalm CXVIII.24 (118:24). Seeing that verse each morning got me off to a better start.

The good smell of coffee and cornbread and the sizzling of bacon cooking on the wood-burning stove hurried me up. I picked up my flannel shirt, boots and socks and ran in and stood by the popping, crackling fire in the fireplace to finish dressing. Mother, in her long blue dress and bright flowered apron, was carrying the milk pitcher and the butter dish to the table.

"How did you sleep last night?" she asked. "I heard your bedsprings do a lot of squeaking."

"I couldn't stop thinking about the test," I told her. "When I finally got to sleep, I kept having dreams. I'll sure be glad when it's all over."

I didn't tell her, but I was really thinking about something else. I had overheard Mother and Dad talking about our money problems. They were talking about not having enough money to live on if the drought continued and the crops failed. There would be no wheat to trade for the things we would need. Mother was working hard at her sewing and Dad was taking odd jobs after the farm chores were done. I decided to start asking around for a job. But I would have to wait until Tuesday. We had to get the planting done first.

I joined Mother and Dad at the table. It was traditional for us to pray before every meal. We took turns and it was Mother's turn that Monday. As she prayed, I sneaked a look at her beautiful face. She seemed to always have a worried expression lately. It made her look older. I really loved her and Dad and I didn't want them to worry about money. I closed my eyes and bowed my head as she finished. She asked for rain and a good crop, and Dad added, "Amen!"

Dad reached across the red and white checkered tablecloth and picked up the plate of bacon and eggs. He helped himself then passed it to me. I took some and handed the plate to Mother. I reached into the oval Indian basket for some corn bread. The bread was so hot that it steamed when I lifted the red and white checkered napkin.

We ate our breakfast in a hurry and with very little talk. We each were anxious to get started. Dad wanted to be in the fields at sunrise, Mother would have to get started on her sewing, and I had my chores to do.

Dad got up and gave Mother a kiss and patted me on the shoulder. He put on his coat and hat and said good-bye. He was so tall that his hat nearly touched the top of the doorway as he walked onto the back porch.

"Be home as soon as possible," he said to me. "We want to finish planting the wheat before the rains come—*if* they come."

Dad was very positive and "if" was a word he seldom used. Mother often assured him that the Lord would provide, but hard times were common and Dad's faith seemed to weaken with each new problem.

I finished my breakfast and gulped down my milk. Mother was still facing the door Dad had just shut, deep in thought.

"I'm going out back to do my chores." My speaking brought her attention back to the kitchen.

"Try to hurry," she said. "You don't want to be late for school." I thought I could see tears beginning to form in her eyes.

Within 25 minutes I had finished stacking the wood and filling the lamps. The sky to the east was beginning to show a brighter red as I headed for the chicken coop. The rooster was sitting on the fence crowing at the sun which hadn't yet risen. He ruffled his feathers reminding me of a hat I had seen in the window of Miss Sophie's Dress Shop. The coop erupted with cackling sounds as I threw a few handsful of feed.

When I came into the kitchen, Mother was standing at the sink doing the dishes. I heard her sniffing and when she turned around I saw that her eyes were red. I pretended not to notice. I grabbed my books and lunch bag from the table.

"Good-bye, Mother," I said as I kissed her cheek.

"Good-bye, Mike," she said with a half smile, "and good luck on your test."

"Thanks!" I shouted as I ran out the front door.

"Don't slam the—" The bang of the door interrupted her instructions.

I ran down our dusty road to the main road that led to town. For over four years, Freddy Baxter, Danny Malone, and Zachery Alexander had met me at the livery stable to begin our walk to school.

The three-mile walk was certainly a long one, but we knew lots of things to do along the way. Even after several years, the journey seemed to present something new every day. *That* day was going to be no exception!

Chapter Two

I was the first one to arrive at the livery stable. I leaned against the fence and watched the horses strolling around inside the large corral. Seeing their breath turn to steam reminded me of fire-breathing dragons. I could imagine the livery stable as some mythical castle with gray towers. A clanking sound from inside the blacksmith's shop quickly interrupted my daydream.

I wondered if Charley, the blacksmith, needed anyone to do odd jobs around the livery stable. I pulled open one of the tall double doors of the shop. Charley was adding coals to his fire and pumping the bellows to make them glow red hot. He was covered by his big leather apron and his sleeves were rolled up above his big muscles. His job for the day was making new branding irons for some of the ranchers in the area. It was always interesting to try to figure out what the different brands stood for.

"Hello, Charley."

"Oh, Mike," he said, "you must be the first one to get here this morning."

"Yes, I am." I was thinking about how to ask him for a job. "May I come in and watch?"

"Sure!"

"Do you need anyone to help with some odd jobs? I would sure like to earn some extra money."

"Nope!" Charley answered quickly and firmly. "I'm afraid you're a bit young and too small for the heavy work around here."

"Well, thanks anyway," I said. I could tell from his firm voice that it wouldn't help to try to talk him into anything. Besides, he was right. I was too small and not very strong.

"I'll see you later, Charley."

I stepped outside and watched the town slowly coming to life. Shopkeepers were arriving at their stores. Mr. Harris, the hotel manager, was sweeping dust from the wooden sidewalks in front of the hotel. Another sign of life was a wagon heading into town from the east. Against the glowing eastern sky it was difficult to see who it was, but I was pretty sure it was Freddy and Mr. Baxter. The wagon came closer and it *was* Freddy and his father. The Baxter farm was more than a mile out of town and Mr. Baxter would bring Freddy in whenever he had the time.

Freddy jumped down from the seat before the wagon rolled to a complete stop. He brushed his bright red hair out of his eyes. The freckles I had were nothing compared to his.

"Good morning, Mr. Baxter."

"Mornin', Mike," he said. "You be home on time this afternoon, Freddy. There's plenty of work to do."

Just then, Danny Malone and Zachery Alexander came around the corner of the depot and across the street. They were good friends but were sure different. Zach's strong, athletic body was more than a head taller and the girls thought he was "so cute!" Danny was homely, chubby, and he never bothered to comb his bushy, light brown hair. They joined us as Mr. Baxter circled his wagon in the road and headed toward home.

We began talking about the geography test we were going to have that day. Freddy and Danny had studied a lot too. Zach, on the other hand, was always playing baseball and said he didn't have time to be bothered with studying.

"Let's get going," said Zach. "What's so special about this test? What good is it going to do us to know all the states anyhow?"

We didn't even try to answer his questions.

The autumn sun rising over the plains warmed our backs a little as we started across the railroad track and up the road. It would take us along Brooks Creek and over the mountain to Pine Ridge. Along the stretch of road at the base of Brooks Peak we could usually hear water rushing in the creek. But the summer had been a dry one. The creek was barely trickling through the bedrocks many feet below the normal water line. There was usually rain by the first of October, but the skies had remained clear and sunny since the beginning of summer. The dust rising from our shuffling feet reminded us of how dry the ground was.

"Pa says it better rain soon or we'll starve next year," said Freddy.

"It will," I said. "We've been praying about it."

"I don't believe that," said Freddy. "Dad says there isn't a God anyhow!"

Danny and I just looked at each other and shrugged. Zach acted as though he hadn't heard a word of our discussion. He thought worrying about God was only for women.

"Well," said Danny, "let's hurry to the Dobson house. I'm going to show you the fine art of stone throwing."

On the previous Friday afternoon we made up a game. The object was to break the glass out of the windows of the old house. Each of us threw once. Danny scored the only hit on Friday by breaking one of the small panes of glass.

Danny bragged, "I'm the leader and plan to remain champ."

"Don't count on leading this contest for long," I told him. "I plan on tying up this game today."

I knew I wouldn't. I purposely missed before by throwing my rock at the front door. I could just imagine what my parents would say about me taking part in such a game. Freddy and Zach knew better too. But they sometimes would do things with Danny that they wouldn't normally do on their own.

The road began its curve to the right. We were coming closer to the house. It had sat empty since the old widow, Mrs. Dobson, died. The fence along the road had begun to lean and its gate was hanging by a single hinge. Most of its white paint had peeled away to reveal the grayish old wood underneath.

We came within sight of the place. The trees along the path to the house drooped to the ground and almost completely hid the house. There were just a few plants struggling to live where Mrs. Dobson's flower bed had been.

"Look, smoke! There's smoke coming from the chimney!" Freddy was talking in an excited whisper. "There's someone in the house. Let's go see who it is!"

We walked closer to the front gate and noticed other signs of life. The broken-out windowpane was boarded over. A pathway had been cleared through the tall weeds to the outhouse in the meadow behind the house. At the side of the house a tired-looking, beige horse stood grazing next to a wagon which held only ropes and tarps that had secured its load.

"I guess our contest is over," said Zach.

"I win!" announced Danny.

"I don't see any broken glass," said Freddy. "Do you, Mike?"

"Nope," I laughed. "I guess Danny didn't break that glass after all!"

Danny didn't think it was funny but the rest of us sure did. I think we were glad too that the contest was over.

"OK, forget it!" Danny scowled. "Let's just find out who's in there. I don't remember hearing any talk of strangers coming to town. Let's flip a coin to see who goes to check it out."

Guess who lost the coin toss.

That's right!

The other boys hid behind some bushes and I sneaked up to the side of the house. As I did I hoped my parents would never hear about what I was doing. I tiptoed along like a cat. The crunching of dry leaves under my feet seemed louder than usual. I crouched down below the window next to the old stone chimney.

A bug buzzed into my ear. I swatted at it and slapped myself on the side of the head. I was afraid I had been heard. I sat there quietly for a few seconds holding my breath. I started to stand up and peek over the windowsill when a sharp noise startled me. The front door squeaked open and somebody with heavy footsteps walked across the porch. I was sure I was caught.

I asked God to forgive me. Then I asked Him to keep me from getting caught, even though I had an idea that wasn't exactly an appropriate prayer.

I wondered if I could sneak away without being seen, so I took a quick glance around the corner.

Facing away from me stood a huge man with a hammer in his hand. He began nailing a loose shutter onto the house. As he finished he turned, and we were face to face. Both of us froze for a second. When I saw his face a chill of fear stood my hair on end. I could feel my heart pounding in my throat. I was so scared I hollered.

The man was yelling something to me as I leaped over some bushes and ran down the path. I ran right through the gate and up the road without looking back.

Chapter Three

I was running from the Dobson house so fast I barely noticed a wagon coming around the bend behind me. I kept on running past the old, abandoned Brooks Gold Mine and around another bend in the road. My feet could hardly keep up with me. Finally my toe hit a high spot in the road. Down I went in a cloud of dust, and my books and lunch bag flew into the tall grass. I looked back along the road to see if anyone was chasing me. There was no one in sight—not even my cowardly friends. I wondered where they could be.

Muffled giggles from behind a nearby bush told where they were. The giggles soon turned to uncontrolled laughter. Some of the laughter seemed a little high-pitched for boys. Danny, Freddy, and Zach had sneaked away from the Dobson house before I even reached the window. They met Christine and Caroline along the road and told them about the excitement.

I just sat there in the road trying to catch my breath. I began to notice the pains caused by my fall. My hands were burning from being scraped along the rough road and I could feel the grit of sand between my teeth. My bloody knee showed through the large hole in my pants. I knew my parents would be unhappy about the condition of my school clothes. I began trying to think of a story to explain how it happened. As I did I remembered what my mother always said about telling a lie: "If you tell one lie, you'll have to tell another. And you'll never be able to remember them all."

"You look like you've seen a ghost," laughed Zach.

"Maybe I did," I said breathlessly.

"Here are your lunch and books," said Christine. Her voice showed some sympathy for me.

"Thanks."

"That's the fastest I've ever seen you run, Mike," laughed Danny.

"Like a scared chicken," added Caroline.

I didn't enjoy being laughed at, so I stood up and began walking on toward school.

"What'd ya see?" asked Freddy.

"If you think it's so funny," I said angrily, "why don't you just go back and find out for yourselves?"

I walked away fast, partly to stay ahead of the laughers and partly out of fear of what I had seen at the Dobson house. What happened next was soon all over town.

The wagon I just got a glimpse of as I ran from the Dobson house was yellow with little pastel flowers. I knew it was Miss Polly's. She painted it herself. Polly Porter's brother was the justice of the peace. She was usually the first person to call at the home of a newcomer to River Junction. Her wagon, called the "Welcome Wagon," was usually packed with little gifts from the townspeople—a jar of Mrs. Collins' famous homemade pickles, some spools of thread from Miss Sophie's Dress Shop, a box of cookies (usually baked by my mother), or perhaps one of Mrs. Dumphy's lopsided chocolate cakes. Sometimes there would be fresh apples from Mr. Brown's trees, a box of fudge from Goodson's Candy Shop, or a ticket for a free meal at the River Junction Hotel.

Whatever she carried in the basket was always accompanied by a lot of town gossip. After 30 minutes with Miss Polly Porter, any outsider would know a great deal about our town. And by the end of the day most of the town would know about the new family.

Miss Polly saw me running from the old Dobson house and got curious. The way I heard about it later, she reckoned she'd better stop and see what I'd been up to. As she pulled up to the house she noticed the smoke rising from the chimney and some movement inside one of the windows. It certainly was unusual for someone to come to town without Miss Polly being aware of it. This was a challenge for her to find out all she could. Even though her wagon was empty, she felt it was her responsibility to call on the newcomers.

As she walked up the path toward the house she noticed the curtains quickly closing. Most people might take that as a hint to come back later, but not Miss Polly. She marched right onto the porch and up to the door. She gave it a healthy knock. There was no answer. Again she knocked.

A deep voice came from within the house,

"Yes?"

"I came to welcome you to River Junction," Miss Polly began. "I know it's early, but I was just passing by and noticed . . ."

"Please—" he tried to speak.

She continued, ". . . there was someone living here."

He tried to talk again, "Perhaps when I—"

She was hard to stop. "I'm Miss Porter, but everyone calls me Miss Polly. I'm the one—"

She stopped as the door squeaked open and her eyes met his. She was so shocked she couldn't move or speak. She stood frozen, looking toward the dark interior of the house and avoided looking directly into the man's face again.

"I'm really not ready for visitors," he said, "but come on in."

The sight of that man changed her mind. "No, I'd best come back later," said Polly nervously.

She began stepping backward across the porch. Her curiosity wanted her to look at his face again, but fear wouldn't let her. Then she bumped into something behind her. The sound of cracking wood told her she had broken something—the porch rail.

"Oh, I'm sorry," said Polly as she turned around to see what she had done.

He stepped onto the porch and reached toward the broken railing. In a deep but gentle voice, he said, "That's OK. I've been working out here this morning. I was going to rebuild that old railing anyway."

Polly tried not to stare at his outstretched hand and arm, and ended up looking him right in the eyes. A chill ran down her neck.

"Good-bye," she said, as she stepped down off

the porch.

"By the way," he raised his voice as she quickly walked away, "my name is Mr. Gehrmann, Edmund Gehrmann."

She didn't say anything. She just walked faster and faster along the pathway toward her wagon. She looked back and saw him still standing on the porch. He waved, but she had already looked away.

Polly climbed up into her wagon and whipped the horse into action. With a "git up" she turned the wagon around and headed back to River Junction. She had forgotten about visiting her friend in Pine Ridge. But Polly had a strange story to tell and she couldn't wait to tell the townspeople.

Chapter Four

I kept right on walking. I was soon out of range of the laughter and tried to forget about the Dobson house and the man I saw there.

I loved this part of the walk to school. The road wound through big, dark oak trees. Their long, spreading branches reached out over the road so that sometimes I had to duck to avoid them. Nothing much else grew along there except grass and little animals. We sometimes chased mice and lizards through the grass and over the rocks. We had to watch for rattlesnakes in warm weather, though. I was nearly bitten by a rattlesnake when I was eight. To this very day I'm scared to death of snakes.

As the road climbed up the side of the hill the oaks mingled with manzanita bushes and pine trees. They got so thick near the top of the hill you couldn't see anything except trees. Then the woods opened up into one large meadow where you could hear animals rustling through the tall grass—if you were real quiet. This morning little puffs of steam rose from the road as the sun melted the frost.

At the other side of the meadow the road crossed over the river where it poured down through a steep gorge. The rough wooden bridge, built by the first white settlers in the area, was now weak from many years of heavy traffic. I watched carefully for loose boards as I walked across.

When the water was higher we had a swimming hole down under the bridge. We used the bridge to dive from. We planned to dam up the water under the bridge to make a bigger and deeper swimming hole. As I looked down into the water I figured we had better do it pretty soon. The rainy season should be starting any day now.

Across the bridge the road climbed higher and the trees grew denser. I breathed in the sweet smell of cedar and pine and pulled my coat around me. The thick shade shut out the sun and it was colder up here. Squirrels squeaked at each other and ran from branch to branch and tree to tree. Birds of many colors and sizes chirped, squawked and twittered from the treetops.

I thought back to what Freddy had said and wondered how anyone could see all these beautiful things of nature and not believe in God.

I walked along, kicking the deep piles of leaves along the roadside. The wind moved through the treetops, sounding like a distant waterfall growing louder and louder. A mysterious silence fell over the forest and the animals stopped their activity. They seemed to sense a change coming. The trees began swaying more and more in the gusty wind. Fluffy clouds drifted across the sky.

I stopped in a clearing at the summit to catch my breath and look at the view. Behind me, way in the distance, I could see the Great Plains, and nestled in the foothills was River Junction.

Smoke rising through a huge clump of oaks marked the location of the Dobson house. A chill went up my spine as I thought about the Dobson house and its new occupant.

Across the valley ahead of me I saw the big red schoolhouse. The name of the town was Pine Ridge. That's also where we went to church. Our schoolhouse and church burned down and hadn't been rebuilt at this time.

Just ahead of me where the road dropped into the small valley Joey, Mary and Louisa Foster came onto the road from a nearby path.

"Hey, Mike," said Joey. "Where are the other musketeers?"

"Oh, they're coming." I changed the subject. "Is that your father chopping down a tree over there?" I could hear the muffled sound of an axe hitting a tree trunk.

"Yes it is," said Mary, in her usual stuck-up manner. "He's filling a *big* order for the lumber mill. He's going to make a *lot* of money."

That girl really made me sick! But her sister, Louisa, was different. I never could understand how those two could be sisters. Louisa was really nice. I didn't dare say that to Danny or Zach. They would have made fun of me. They always pretended they didn't want to have anything to do with girls.

Louisa was a year younger than I was. She had big blue eyes and long, light brown hair. I knew she would be the first girl I would ask to the Saturday night square dance. That would be when my parents said I was old enough.

From somewhere inside the woods we could hear Mr. Foster shout, "Timber!" Then came the crunching sound as the tree began its fall to the earth. The tall sugar pine swished through the air and hit the ground with a loud rumble. The ground shook and a huge cloud of dust rose through the trees.

"We'd better get going," said Louisa, "or we might be late."

We continued walking toward school.

"Are you ready for the states test?" asked Mary.

"Yeah, how about you?" I said. I knew Mary was ready. She was a straight-A student and she let everyone know it whenever she had a chance. I didn't even listen for her answer.

We could see Miss Hartfield standing on the front porch pulling the rope that ran up to the bell tower. The school bell began to clang out its warning. School would begin in 10 minutes. We were expected to always be "prompt." We hurried along the road. By the time we came to the baseball field next to the school, our group had increased in size. The main topic of discussion was the geography test.

"I always get Illinois and Indiana mixed up," said Ralph. "Which is to the east and which one is to the west?"

"Just remember," said Mary, with her nose in the air. "Indiana has the word 'Indian' in it. Of course, when you think of Indians, you think of the west. Indiana is the one to the west."

I stopped to think about what she had said. That wasn't right! It was backwards. Illinois is the state to the west. Mary actually made a mistake? I didn't say anything.

"Thanks," said Ralph.

"Oh, it was nothing," said Mary, looking down her nose.

"Hey, Ralph," I whispered after Mary walked away, "that's wrong. She has them backwards. Illinois is the state to the west."

"Sure, Mike," he said doubtingly. "Mary always gets A's. Why should I believe you?"

The final bell cut short our conversation. We quietly filed up the stairs and into the coatroom. I put my lunch on the shelf and hung my coat on one of the hooks. Danny, Freddy, Zach, and the girls were coming up the steps behind me. On the left of the coatroom was the boys' washroom. The girls' was on the right. Wash was all you could do there. There were two outhouses under a huge oak tree behind the schoolhouse. They each had four doors and the same number of seats.

The schoolhouse was a big two-story building. One big room on the first floor was for those of us in the first eight grades. Upstairs, the older students had their classes. I used to wonder if that was where they got the name "high school."

We walked quietly from the coatroom into the main classroom and stood beside our desks. Miss Hartfield stood behind her desk and watched us enter the room. She wasn't the best looking woman. Her hair was always drawn up in a huge bun on top of her head and her glasses made her look even stranger. But that smile that greeted us made me feel that she truly cared about each and every one of us.

The first thing we did was say a short prayer and then the flag salute. Joey had been chosen that week to give the order, "Ready, salute."

All together we said, "I pledge allegiance to my flag and to the Republic for which it stands, one nation, indivisible, with liberty and justice for all."

"Good morning, class."

"Good morning, Miss Hartfield," we answered together.

Everyone sat down and Miss Hartfield took the roll. That didn't take long because she could see that all the desks were filled. Thinking of those hard wooden seats still makes my back ache. They came only in two sizes: too small and too big. Each desk top was connected to the seat in front of it. There was a hole in the upper right-hand corner to hold an ink bottle and a shelf underneath for our books.

"Well, class," said Miss Hartfield, "it's time for the big test. Get your pens ready and clear off your desks." Her words brought a bunch of groans from us.

The tests were passed out face down. The test paper was a blank map of the United States that Miss Hartfield had Mr. Simpson make up in his printing shop.

"You have 20 minutes to finish," she began her instructions. "There is to be no talking and keep your eyes on your own paper. Begin." She said the very same thing before every test as though we had never heard it before.

My studying paid off. I filled in my map quickly and had plenty of time to check it over. Then I began to daydream. Out of the windows on my right I could see the town of Pine Ridge. It was busy with the activity of early morning: people and wagons moving about, smokestacks and chimneys puffing out billows of smoke. Through the windows on my left I had a beautiful view of the forest-covered mountains. There was no snow yet on the high peaks. I sat leaning against my hand as I dreamt on.

Thoughts about that morning were interrupted as a hand grabbed my shoulder tightly. It was Miss Hartfield's.

"What do you think you're doing, Michael?" said an angry Miss Hartfield. "How dare you look at Mary's paper! I'll see you after school today and you can take a note home to your parents."

I guess I was looking *toward* her paper, but I wasn't looking *at* it. I tried to explain that I was just staring off into distance, "But, I—"

"We'll talk about this *after* school." She didn't give me a chance to explain.

What made it even worse was the fact that it was Mary's paper I was accused of copying. It almost made me sick when she wrinkled up her nose and upper lip at me, like she was a queen and I was a thief.

I don't remember exactly what we did the rest of the day. I was just hoping the day would be over and I could go home. But normally we would read from our McGuffey's Readers, do our arithmetic problems, practice our handwriting, and study government or history.

The school day finally ended and Miss Hartfield dismissed the class. She asked me to come to her desk. As the rest of the class reached the front steps, the building rumbled with the sound of running feet.

Miss Hartfield was sitting at her desk. Behind her was the chalkboard. Above the chalkboard was the United States flag and a picture of George Washington.

I looked up at the picture of our first president. I wondered what would have happened if Miss Hartfield had caught him chopping down a cherry tree.

"I'm disappointed in you, Michael. Take this note home and discuss it with your parents."

"Please, Miss Hartfield, let me—" I tried to explain.

"Let's not talk about it anymore young man," she interrupted. "I'll be expecting a note tomorrow morning. You may go on home now." She stood and turned away from me.

As she began erasing the blackboard I stood there for a moment thinking that she wasn't herself that day. I didn't try to say anything more. I turned and walked out of the room and down the steps. The only other students still around were the ones playing baseball.

The puffy white clouds had turned gray and were growing larger. They were blocking out the sun but the air had become warmer and humid. That usually meant rain was not far away.

"Mike!"

I was surprised to hear my dad's voice. He was sitting in the wagon waiting for me to get out of school.

"Hi, Dad!" I said as I jammed the note into my hip pocket.

"You're a little late getting out," he said.

"Yeah, I was talking to Miss Hartfield," I said. "What are you doing here?"

"I had to pick up more seed in Pine Ridge," he said, "and I thought you'd like a ride home."

"I sure would," I answered. "But if it's alright with you, I'll ride in the back. Those sacks look like good pillows and I could sure use a nap."

"Sure, Mike, rest a little. We have quite a bit of work to get done at home. It looks like we might get rain tonight or tomorrow." He talked in a serious tone, "We sure need it, but we've got to get the rest of the seed in the ground first. I hope it holds off until then."

I was surprised at first that he hadn't asked about the geography test, but I knew he had things on his mind. I was also glad because I wasn't ready to explain what had happened in school.

The gunny sacks did make a great bed and the movement of the wagon over the bumpy road soon rocked me to sleep. Pine Ridge was pretty quiet compared to what was going on in River Junction.

Chapter Five

By mid-afternoon, Miss Polly's story about the Dobson house was all over town. Each time it became a little more scary and a little less accurate.

The first stop Miss Polly made when she returned to town that morning was at Sophie's Dress Shop. Polly thought of Sophie as her best friend. Sophie didn't think of Polly in the same way, but she was always nice to her. Sophie did enjoy hearing the latest gossip though, especially the way Miss Polly could tell it.

My mom was in Sophie's Dress Shop when Miss Polly came in. Mom had dropped in to buy sewing thread. Sophie was busy helping Doctor Powell's wife pick out a new dress.

"You wouldn't believe what happened," Polly began. Miss Sophie ignored Polly while she waited on Mrs. Powell.

"Hello, Mrs. Roberts," said Polly. "You'll never guess what I saw this morning at the old Dobson house."

"How are you, Polly?" Mother asked.

"I saw Michael near the Dobson house," began Polly. "I guess he was on his way to school."

"By himself?" asked Mother. "Weren't the other boys with him?"

"No," Polly quickly returned to trying to tell her story. "You won't believe what I saw!"

Everyone in the shop stopped and listened as Polly told her detailed story. Even Mrs. Powell gave Polly her undivided attention. Nobody noticed that Mrs. Alexander had come into the shop too.

Mother got in her question just as Polly finished. "Where did you say you saw Mike?"

"He was running up the road toward school," said Miss Polly.

"I guess he was alright," Mother thought out loud. "He was probably just trying to catch up with the boys."

The discussion continued about the stranger in town.

"How could it be that such a horrible man would be living in the Dobson place?" asked Mrs. Alexander.

"I wonder if he's supposed to be there," Sophie added.

"I didn't hear about that old house being sold to anyone," said Polly.

As the others continued talking, Mother sat there thinking that something different had happened that day. And she had a feeling I was involved in some way.

The way I heard it, in just a few minutes Mrs.

Alexander made her way to the General Store
(which used to be the Dobsons' store) where she
began telling the story. Emily Collins, who worked
on the newspaper, the *Expositor*, heard the story.
She wanted to get all the details, so she set out for
the courthouse to find Miss Polly. Since Polly's
brother was the justice of the peace the courthouse seemed to be a logical place to start looking.
Sure enough, Miss Polly was standing at the bot-
tom of the courthouse steps talking to my mom
who had walked out of the store with her. Emily
came across the street.

"I heard your story," Emily said, "and I want
some more details for the paper. Are you alright?"

"Oh, sure, I'm fine," Miss Polly replied. "I was
just scared a little." Polly was excited at the
thought that she might get her name in the paper.

"What did the sheriff say about it?" asked
Emily.

"I didn't think I needed to tell him."

Emily knew better than to believe stories that
had been passed along from one person to
another. She asked Polly to tell her story. Polly's
description of what happened was not as exaggerated when she knew it might be printed in the
newspaper.

"Did it look like he was actually *living* there?"

"The house looked very lived-in," answered
Miss Polly. "There was a fire in the fireplace, and
there were new curtains and some furniture. He
was even making repairs on the front stoop."

"It's funny, though," said Emily, "that this man
would come to town without anyone knowing a
thing about him. What did the justice say?"

"Clifford said he didn't know a thing about it,"
said Polly. "But he's going to look into it. You know

how most folks around here feel about someone coming into town unannounced."

"Who owns that old house?"

"I don't know," answered Polly. "When Mrs. Dobson died there were no heirs."

"Well, thanks, Polly. I think there's more to this story. If he's hiding something, I'll find out what it is." Mother left the two ladies then and went back home. She had a lot to think about.

The story changed many times that day as it spread through town. Charley, the blacksmith, told me he heard that the man grabbed Miss Polly and shoved her against the railing. She got away and he chased her to her wagon. She just barely escaped. You know how stories get changed when they're told a lot.

Chapter Six

The wagon jolted and rattled as it rolled over the railroad tracks, and that was the end of my nap. We were entering River Junction from the west. I sat up to see what was going on in the town. By that time of the afternoon, there was a great deal of activity on the main street.

In 50 years, River Junction had grown from an isolated stagecoach way station to a busy little farming town. The stables and the stagecoach depot—now also the train depot—sitting across from each other, were the first buildings. The foreman of the stagecoach depot, Anthony Brooks—we called him Tony—was responsible for much of the early building done in River Junction. He was the one who had surveyed the area and personally selected the site.

It was here that the westward trail began its climb over the mountains. Tony knew that travelers would welcome a resting place before starting that difficult journey. He also knew that the two rivers which joined nearby would bring in the business of the mountain people. He predicted the coming of the railroad and the development of the land into farms. River Junction existed in the mind of Tony Brooks long before the first boards were nailed together. Tony's mark was left on the map. The smaller river to the north, a local mountain peak, and the county were named in his honor.

In the 1890s River Junction still had the flavor of the Gold Rush days. The dusty roads leading north and west had two deep ruts from years of wagon traffic. The very fancy hotel and saloon also stood as reminders of the many bags of gold dust which were quickly spent. But the town had settled to a more relaxed pace. The hotel was seldom full and the saloon served mostly local farmers who were tired and thirsty from a full day's work.

The "three o'clock" train was sitting at the depot as we entered town. We called it the "three o'clock" because that was the time it was supposed to be there. Often, though, it would arrive by noon or as late as dinner time. The steam engine was being filled with the water supply necessary for its trip over the high mountains. The old wooden water tower was a huge one. Its big round tank was fed by a huge pipe running from the river.

"The train's in, Dad," I said. "Let's watch it leave!"

"OK, I have to get something in the depot," he said. "But we have to hurry home. We can't wait very long."

The freight car had been unloaded. Boxes from many points in the east were stacked on the platform, awaiting their owners. There were boxes of clothing for Sophie's Dress Shop, large spools of barbed wire, mail sacks, and a stack of newspapers from St. Louis and other major cities. We got all the important news over the telegraph, but there were few details. Most people in town bought the newspapers to read about the Spanish-American War. It had begun in February when the battleship Maine was sunk in the harbor of Havana, Cuba. The papers said there was no proof of who did it, but many Americans were angry at Spain and war was declared. It was in the papers that we first learned about a man named Roosevelt and his "Rough Riders." We hoped that the next shipment of newspapers would bring us more details.

The freight car had been reloaded with products from the local area. One flat car had a tall stack of lumber from the Pine Ridge Mill.

Most of the passengers had returned to their seats from their rest stop inside the depot. One new passenger, Harold Dixon, bought his ticket and boarded the train. Dad said Harold, age 20, was setting out to San Francisco to find a job.

When Grandpa was visiting us he told us many stories about San Francisco. He was there in the busy days of the Gold Rush. He talked about the ocean and the hundreds of ships that sailed into and out of the big harbor. The ships were so thick, he claimed, that a man could walk clear across the bay by jumping from deck to deck. I was almost sure his stories were exaggerated, but I still enjoyed hearing them. I had dreams of seeing that big city. But most of all, I wanted to see the Pacific Ocean and those big sailing ships.

My daydreams of San Francisco, the ocean, and sailing ships were interrupted by the excited, loud blast of the train's whistle.

The conductor called in a deep, booming voice, "All aboooooard!"

He waved his red handkerchief at the engineer. The engine backed up slowly to get a running start at pulling all the weight behind it. Then it started forward with its wheels spinning and then grabbing. Slowly the train moved away from the depot, chug-chug-chug-chug-chug. Another blast from the whistle warned that it would cross the road.

The departure of the train always brought out a great many people who waved to the passengers. They waved as though they really knew the people and were telling them good-bye. Mr. and Mrs. Dixon were there to tell Harold good-bye. Everyone in the crowd was waving or cheering as the train pulled out. Well, almost everyone. Mrs. Dixon was just standing there, crying.

Dad and Mr. Hammond came out of the freight room of the depot carrying a large crate. The crate was marked with a big "S" and the word "Singer."

"I think we can fit it behind the seat," said Dad. "Thanks, Al."

"I hope she gets good use out of it," said Al.

"What is it, Dad?"

"It's a surprise," he said. "Here, take the reins. You can drive us home."

"What is it?" I asked again.

"I told you, it's a surprise." Dad had a grin on his face. I knew he would tell me if I begged him.

"Please, tell me what it is."

"If you promise not to tell, I'll tell you," he said.

"I promise!"

"It's a sewing machine," he said. "I ordered it a long time ago for our wedding anniversary. It came a bit late, but I'm sure she won't mind that."

"She'll really be surprised," I told Dad. "I've seen her looking at them in the mail-order catalogue. She said it would sure help her get a lot of sewing done. But she said we couldn't afford one."

Before I could ask, he said, "You let *me* worry about that!"

The livery stable was bustling with excitement as we went by. Some of the ranchers had brought their horses in for branding and breaking. A crowd was gathering to watch the cowboys try their skills at taming the bucking broncos.

We turned the corner and our house was in sight. Our farm stretched north and east of the house. In the distance the faint sound of the train whistle echoed through the hills. The wind was picking up, swirling dust, golden leaves and tumbleweeds across the road. The clouds grew larger and darker, especially over the mountains.

We pulled up in front of the house and could see a large crew of men out in the fields planting seed. There were a few hired hands but mostly friends who just volunteered to help with the planting. Mr. Foster was there too. He helped in exchange for Dad helping him with logging the next day.

"You go in and change into your work clothes," said Dad, "and I'll get back to work."

I ran into the house. Mother was sitting there in her rocking chair working on her sewing. I thought about the many hours she spent sitting in that chair and working. I had to try hard to keep from smiling when I thought about the surprise.

"Hi!" I ran over and gave her a kiss and hurried to my room to get changed.

Without looking up from her sewing, she said,

"I've been anxious to hear about how you did on the test."

I hesitated and then said, "I think I answered all of them."

"Oh, I'm sure you did," she said. "You knew them all very well last night."

That reminded me about the note. I decided to wait to show it to her. Besides, I was in a hurry to get out into the field. Well, I wasn't really, but that gave me an excuse to hurry outside.

As I headed for the door, my mother said, "I talked to Miss Polly today. She said she saw you on the way to school, near the Dobson house. She had a rather interesting story to tell."

"Dad's waiting for me," I interrupted, "so I have to go."

I opened the door and I could hear Mother say, "We can talk about it when you and your father come in for dinner."

"Oh, no!" I thought. "Miss Polly must have seen me running from the Dobson house." I wondered how much she knew and how much she had told my mother.

The big black clouds were now blocking the sun. The wind was warmer and it was raising swirls of dust from the freshly-plowed field. I ran past the chicken coop and the barn. Dad and the other men were already at work in the fields.

"Mike, you drive one of the wagons." Dad shouted his orders to me and the others.

Some of the men sat in the back of the wagons throwing out the seed. Other men followed on horses dragging huge rakes to cover the seed. The gusting wind made the job very uncomfortable. It was difficult to see and breathe when a cloud of dust rolled over the wagon. We wore red bandanas that made us look like bank robbers, but we could still feel the grit in our teeth and eyes. The next few hours seemed like days.

We finished as the sun was dropping below the clouds on its way to setting behind the mountains. Big swirls of dust rose from the planted field like tiny tornadoes.

Dad stood at the edge of the field next to the barn. The smile on his face showed he was pleased with the job we had done. "Now it can rain," he said. "Let's get this equipment into the barn."

In the distance a rumble of thunder could be heard over the sound of the wind.

We put our horse into its stall and pushed the wagon into the barn. Dad laughed as I took off my hat and bandana. When he took off his, I could see why he was laughing. We both looked like raccoons.

We put the empty feed sacks in a pile and then we fed the horse. I looked around to see where Dad had put Mother's surprise.

Before I even asked, he said, "It's up in the loft. We can come back out tonight and put it together."

"Yeah, then she can start using it tomorrow!"

"I'm starved," said Dad. "How about you?"

"I sure am!"

The last rays of the sun were lighting the bottoms of the high clouds with a bright orange-red tint. We walked toward the house. I began to think about the events of the day and the note I would have to show my parents. My appetite began to disappear as my stomach tightened.

How would I explain that note?

Chapter Seven

The depot, as we called it, was only the waiting room of the train station which we used as a public meeting place. Most of the townspeople probably didn't even realize that "depot" came from the French word for station. The tradition of meeting at the depot started many years before when the oldest men of the town would sit around the pot-bellied stove to talk. As the years went by, more and more people would join at the depot to listen to the stories being exchanged there. The four oldest men of the town would take their seats of honor around the stove and all the other men would sit or stand wherever there was a place—the wooden benches, the front windowsill, or even the floor. Sometimes they just leaned against a wall.

Not only was the depot a good place to hear what was going on, it was a good place to see what was going on. From the front window we could see the main street, the hotel, and the general store. It was especially handy for looking over new people coming in on the train behind the depot or on the stage out front.

The depot was kept in fine shape by Andy Brooks and his son, Cliff. It was always clean and freshly painted in beige with dark brown trim. The two brass chandeliers hanging from the ceiling were kept bright and shiny. The candles were usually burned only on special occasions because they were not easily replaced. Light was provided by the kerosene lanterns on the walls. Cliff cleaned the fancy glass shades and filled them each day so they would be ready for any late night discussions.

Just inside the front door of the depot was the caged window of the ticket and telegraph office. On the wall beside the window was a blackboard. The telegraph operator, Otis Hawkins, kept it up to date with all the latest information on incoming trains and stages.

On that October night, the crowd was gathering early at the depot—including Freddy, who told me what went on. He was there with his dad. The four chairs around the stove were occupied by Mr. Collins, Mr. Bishop, Mr. Brooks, and Mr. Davenport. Mr. Strump, the manager of the General Store, had also come in. As more and more people finished dinner, the depot became quite crowded.

Willy Collins was the oldest of the four men around the stove. He was the father-in-law of Emily Collins. He had started the newspaper, the *Expositor*, many years before. His son, Wally, took over the business, and Wally's wife, Emily, soon became its number one reporter.

Andy Brooks was the second oldest and the son of Tony Brooks. He was the very first baby born in

River Junction. During the Gold Rush he went to California. It was there that he met Thomas Bishop. They became very close friends and came to River Junction together after they failed to make their fortunes in the Golden State.

Thomas Bishop, the third of the four elders, had other reasons for leaving California. There were too many bad memories there. He had married a young lady from Columbia, but she died when she gave birth to their first child. Unfortunately, the child, a boy, died too. Tom said he would never be able to return to California.

Mr. Davenport was not as old as the other three men, but he was the oldest bachelor in River Junction. He was known by most people as Sleepy Charlie. He was given the nickname because he often nodded off, even during the most interesting and lively discussions.

The discussion that night was a lively one indeed.

"What do you know about this stranger who's living out there at the Dobson house?" asked Willy Collins.

"I don't like it when someone sneaks into town like that," said Tom Bishop. "What's he got to hide anyway?"

"Maybe he's afraid to be seen because of the way he looks," said Mr. Strump.

"What's wrong with the way he looks?" asked Willy. "Has anyone seen him?"

"Miss Polly was out there today," replied Joe. "She said his face was a frightening sight."

"What did it look like?" someone asked from across the room.

"Polly didn't say," replied Joe. "Well, actually, I didn't talk to her myself. I heard Mrs. Alexander telling the story at the General Store while I was waiting on another customer."

The door opened and in walked Martin Albright. He was the best lawyer in town. Actually, until 1892, he was the only lawyer in town. That's when a young lawyer from San Francisco set up an office in town to give him some competition.

A few heads turned when he entered—except for Mr. Davenport's. His head dropped to his chest as he fell asleep sitting up in his chair. The conversation continued.

"I hear tell he wasn't too kind to Miss Polly," said Mr. Baxter. "He chased her away from the Dobson house when she was only trying to be nice."

"Are you guys talking about Mr. Gehrmann, the man who bought the Dobson house?" asked Martin Albright.

"Yeah," said Tom. "What do you know about him?"

"Well, perhaps more than I should tell you," answered Martin. "His lawyer—"

"His lawyer?" interrupted Willy.

"Yes," continued Martin, "his lawyer set up the purchase of the house."

"You mean he's some rich city slicker?" asked Tom.

"I know he's from San Francisco," answered Martin, "and I have an idea he's got a lot of money."

"If he's wealthy why didn't he buy a better house here in town?" The question came from someone sitting in the front windowsill.

"Yeah," Willy added, "why would he want to buy that rundown old place?"

"I think that's really his business," said Martin,

"and he did it all legally."

"I still think we should have the sheriff check up on him," came a voice from near the front door.

"Yeah," a few others agreed.

"You can't do that!" Martin raised his voice. "He hasn't done anything wrong, as far as we know. Maybe he just wants some privacy."

"What do you know about the way he looks?" asked Tom.

"Well, I've never met him face to face," said Martin, "and his lawyer didn't say anything about it."

"What about what he did to Miss Polly?" asked Mr. Baxter.

"How many of you have talked to Miss Polly *personally* since this morning?"

Mr. Baxter offered his version of the story. "My wife said she talked to Mrs. Stanley and she had talked to Mrs. Alexander—"

"Sounds to me like news through the grapevine," interrupted Martin. "You men know how stories become twisted and exaggerated after they've been passed around this town all day."

"Well, Emily's going out there to get the story tomorrow," said Willy. "My daughter-in-law will find out what he's up to."

"She'd better take the sheriff with her," said Mr. Baxter.

"That won't be necessary," said Martin. "If he had really done any harm to Miss Polly, don't you think she would have told the sheriff right away?" Martin's logical, legal mind always provided a balance when everyone else was letting their feelings do the talking.

"Well, I guess so," admitted Willy.

"How about if I go out there tomorrow afternoon and talk with him?" asked Martin. "I'll tell him your concerns and maybe I'll have something to tell you. OK?"

Most of the men nodded in agreement.

The discussion seemed to stir Mr. Davenport. With a snort Charlie awoke from his nap. "Hello, Martin, come on in and sit down."

Everyone laughed at Charlie but he didn't seem to mind. He just went back to sleep.

Chapter Eight

Dad and I entered the house from the back porch. We came through the squeaky back door and could smell the pot roast and freshly baked bread.

"Mmmmm, it sure smells good," said Dad.

I nodded and smiled to him. The food did smell good, but I was wondering what Mother would say about what happened at the Dobson house.

We both went over to get a kiss from Mother. She was standing at the sink, pumping water. The pump handle squeaked and the water gurgled out and into the kettle. She gave us a peck of a kiss as though she was kissing a dead fish.

"You men look like you've been rolling on the ground," she said. I always liked it when she said, "you men." "How about getting yourselves cleaned up while I finish the dinner?"

I went into my room to change. I wondered

when the questions were going to begin. I returned to the kitchen to wash up. Dad was pumping water into a washbowl. He added some hot water from a pan on the stove. By the time we finished washing, the water was nearly mud.

Mother was sitting at the work table in the middle of the kitchen, shucking corn. "How did the planting go?"

"It was really windy and dusty, but we got it planted," Dad answered. "I just hope we get some rain to settle the soil before the wind blows the seed away."

"It's been trying to storm all day," said Mother as she dropped the corn into the boiling water.

"Yeah," said Dad, "it looks like the mountains are really getting some rain."

There was a quiet pause as all conversation stopped.

"Well, dinner is cooking," said Mother, "and before we eat we have something to talk about."

Oh, no, I thought. *Here it comes!*

Mother looked at me and a frown had begun to form on her face. She glanced at Dad and back at me. I began counting the squares on the checkerboard tablecloth.

"What is it?" Dad asked. I didn't look up but I could feel him looking at me.

"Michael," Mother said. "You tell us what happened."

I started to explain, "We just wanted to see who was there—"

"Where?" Dad interrupted.

"At the Dobson house," I continued. "I lost the coin toss so I was the one who had to go up to the window and see—"

I was interrupted again, this time by Mother. "I

don't think we're talking about the same thing."

Dad asked quickly, "What were you doing at the Dobson house?"

"Wait just a minute." Mother pulled a small piece of paper from her apron and continued, "I'm talking about this note. It says Michael was cheating on his geography test."

"What?!" Dad was frowning at me now.

"Let me explain—" I began.

"Yes, you better explain," said Dad, "and then you can tell us what happened at the Dobson house."

My voice was shaky. "Maybe I should tell you about the Dobson house and *then* school."

I told them about seeing someone in the Dobson house, the coin toss, spying at the window, the man coming out, the way he looked, and how I ran away.

"That explains how your good school pants were torn," said Mother in a disgusted tone of voice.

Then I explained how I was daydreaming and how Miss Hartfield thought I was looking at Mary's paper.

Spssssssh. The water boiled over and Mother walked over to take the kettle off the stove.

"Son, why didn't you tell me when I picked you up at school?" Dad asked.

"I didn't think you had time. I really wasn't trying to hide anything." I stopped to take a deep breath. "I planned on giving you the note after dinner."

Dad asked, "And were you also planning on telling us about what you did at the Dobson house?"

I hesitated and then answered, "No, not really." That reminded me that I hadn't told them about the rock throwing we had done on Friday. But I decided that it wasn't the time to be totally honest.

"Michael," Mother said firmly. "I guess you know some kind of punishment is called for."

"But I didn't cheat on the test!"

"Your mother and I realize that, Michael. We can talk about that later with Miss Hartfield. What bothers us is that you weren't honest with us. So you'll be punished for that. You need to apologize to the man tonight."

"Not tonight, please, Dad!"

"Yes, tonight," he squinted his eyes to show he wanted no argument. "We'll go right after dinner!"

"No, Dad, please," I said. "I'm afraid to."

"That's ridiculous. He didn't try to hurt you." Dad's voice was getting stronger. "Just because he looks different doesn't mean you should be afraid of him." I got the feeling he was trying to convince himself too.

"But, Dad—" I tried to talk him out of it.

"Let's not talk about it anymore." Dad's voice was about as loud as I had ever heard it. "We're going out there right after dinner *and that's final!*"

"And because you weren't honest with us," added Mother, "you'll come straight home after school for the rest of this week."

I guess the punishment was fair enough, but I sure didn't think so at the time. I was wondering how I could find time to look for a job. I couldn't tell my parents because they would tell me I didn't need to work. They thought I had enough to do with my chores and my school work.

I just sat there thinking over all that had happened that day. Mother removed the checkered tablecloth from the table and replaced it with a linen tablecloth that had belonged to my grand-mother.

I got up without saying anything. I helped set the table and sat back down at my place. Mother set the pot roast, fresh bread, string beans, and corn on the cob on the table across from me. Then she sat down to my right and Dad to my left. We joined hands as Dad said the blessing.

"Our Father, we thank you for your blessings and for the food on our table. We pray that you will bring the rain to make our crops grow. In Jesus' name, Amen."

Dad's prayers weren't always fancy, but they were sincere.

We passed the food and served our plates with only polite talk. I didn't want to eat. Thinking about going back to the Dobson house and seeing that man had taken my appetite away. We had a very quiet dinner. I guess we had all talked enough.

And I thought, *After this mess is settled, I have to get things straightened out with Miss Hartfield.* I wondered how such a good boy could get himself into so much trouble in one day.

Chapter Nine

"Come on, Mike," said Dad, "finish your dinner. We've got to get over to the Dobson house so you can apologize."

"I'm not hungry."

"OK, let's go now then," he said.

"Please, Dad, not tonight."

Dad didn't say anymore. I could tell by the look on his face that I better not either.

Mother said, "You better take your raincoats."

Dad started out the back door. He gave Mother a kiss and the door banged shut behind him. I started out the door after him.

"Do I get a kiss from you too?" Mother asked.

"Sure." I gave her a sloppy one.

"Don't worry," she said, "you have nothing to be afraid of. Your dad will be with you." I've noticed that people often say "there's nothing to be afraid of" when there really is.

We went to the barn to hitch the wagon. Lightning flashed over the mountains and the rumbling thunder rolled across the sky. Dad slid the wooden bolt back and pulled the heavy barn door open.

"Light the lantern," said Dad, "and we'll take it with us. It'll be dark on the Creek Road."

We walked the horse from its stall and hitched it to the wagon. Neither one of us said anything more. I climbed into the seat and held the lantern. Dad shook the reins to get the horse to move out of the barn. When the wagon cleared the barn he put on the brake and went back to shut the door.

Dad climbed into the seat beside me, shook the reins again, and told the horse to "git." We pulled around to the front of our house. We could see the lights of the main street of River Junction. The livery stable was dark and only a few horses moved around inside the main corral. They seemed very uneasy about the weather. As we neared the stable, the side door swung open and out came Charley, the blacksmith. He chased the horses toward the open door and inside. It closed quickly behind him.

The sounds from the depot echoed across the main street and Dad commented, "It sounds like quite a wild meeting in there."

The wind rustled through the leaves along the edge of the road. Every so often, a lonely raindrop would hit me in the face. For an October night it was fairly warm. We really didn't need our lantern because the flashes of lightning were doing a good job of lighting our way.

Even after we drove over the railroad crossing we could hear the hum of activity from the depot. But the voices were soon drowned out by the wind and thunder.

The ride seemed so very short. Too short. We soon came around the bend in the road and could see the lights from inside the Dobson house. Small sparks blowing into the air marked the place where the chimney stood. The house was so surrounded by trees that the lightning just barely lit it.

We pulled up by the picket fence and tied the horse to a post. The gusting wind stirred up a pile of dry leaves. The low-hanging branches of the trees scraped back and forth along the ground and across the path. The small gate banged with each gust of wind.

"Do you want to go in alone?" asked Dad.

"No!" I nearly died at the thought of going in alone. "You come with me!"

Our feet were nearly buried in the deep layer of leaves as we walked toward the front porch. Our boots made loud thumping noises as we walked up the steps and across the porch.

Dad knocked.

We could hear footsteps inside coming closer and closer to the front door.

"Who's there?" came the deep voice from inside.

"Tell him," Dad ordered.

"It's Michael Roberts." I knew he didn't know who I was, but I couldn't think of anything else to say.

"Who?"

"I'm the one who was here this morning. My dad and I came to talk to you."

The door opened slowly. I didn't look up. I was afraid to see that face again. The man extended his hand to my dad and they shook hands. Dad tried to act as though nothing was unusual, but I could tell he was surprised by what he saw.

"Hello, I'm Dave Roberts."

"I'm Ed Gehrmann," the man said. "Did your son say his name is Mike?"

"Yes, and he's here to apologize for disturbing you this morning."

"That's quite alright," said Mr. Gehrmann. "I think we startled each other. My face has scared away a lot of people lately."

Dad and I stood there motionless. We didn't know if we should laugh or say something. I looked up at him and his face didn't seem so awful anymore.

"Don't be embarrassed," he said. "I've seen all sorts of reactions from people. I can understand how it must be to look at my face for the first time. As bad as it is, I guess I've gotten used to it."

We were still standing there silently. I wanted to know what had happened to him, but I knew it wouldn't be polite to ask.

"Please come in and sit down, if you can find a place among all of these crates and boxes."

"We can't stay long," said Dad.

The parlor was unlike anything I had ever seen. There were clocks in every possible place. The ticking noises filled the room. It was very easy to see that it was almost nine o'clock.

Dad poked me in the shoulder. "What do you have to say to Mr. Gehrmann?"

"I'm sorry about spying on you, Mr. Gehrmann."

"That's OK, Michael." He had an unusual smile on his face. "The subject is closed."

At the next moment it was nine o'clock and the house began erupting with the sounds of the clocks. They rang, dinged, chimed, bonged,

clanged, and cuckooed. It was an incredible sight
to see those clocks all working together. After
about two or three minutes, they stopped.

"Wow!" I said. "Isn't it hard to keep them all
working together?"

"It sure is," said Mr. Gehrmann as a lonely
clock struck *six* times. "It's also difficult to keep
them working *correctly*."

We all laughed and still another clock chimed.

"As you can see," he said, "I still have some
work to do on some of them."

"How long have you been a clockmaker?" Dad
asked.

"It's mostly a hobby," he said. "In San Francisco our clock tower had an old clock that often
quit. So I tried to fix it. I was as surprised as everyone else when the clock worked and continued to
work.

"A few people brought their clocks to me to see
what I could do with them. I studied books and
fixed more and more.

"Pretty soon I had so many clocks that I had no
place to keep them. So I decided to open a shop.
When I had the time to get away from my work, I
would work in the clock shop. The people in the
neighborhood even started calling me 'Father
Time.' "

He stopped for a moment. He stood and walked
over to the fireplace and began winding one of the
mantel clocks.

He continued his story facing away from us.
"Then came the accident. After I had been in the
hospital for quite some time, people came to visit.
Many of them suggested I might stay with them for
a while after I got out of the hospital. But the offers
were never repeated after I was allowed to leave. I

guess they felt uneasy about having me around
their families and friends because of the way I
looked."

Boom! A crash of thunder shook the house.

"I knew I would have to give up my primary pro-
fession," he continued. "You see, looking the way I
do I couldn't face so many people."

I wondered what kind of work Mr. Gehrmann
had done where he had to face a lot of people.

Another clap of thunder shook the house.

Mr. Gehrmann wiped his eyes before he turned
around to face us again. "Well, it sounds like quite
a storm building up out there."

"Yes," Dad spoke up quickly, "we should get
going. It's going to pour before we get home."

"Thanks for coming. It was nice to have someone to talk to," said Mr. Gehrmann.

"Dad, could we stay just a little longer?" I
asked. "I want to hear some more stories about
San Francisco."

"No, it's getting late and you have school tomorrow."

"How about coming back tomorrow, Michael,
and I'll tell you all sorts of stories about San Francisco?"

"Sure!" I said. Then I remembered. "Oh, I
can't."

"Mike has to go directly home every day this
week," said Dad. "It's punishment for his poor
behavior."

"Well, maybe next week?"

"Great, I'll be here!"

He opened the door and we walked out onto the
porch. It was beginning to rain so we said our
good-byes and ran to the wagon.

"Git up!"

"Dad, what kind of job do you think he was talking about?"

"I don't know. I got the feeling he was trying *not* to tell us. It sounded very important to him. It must have hurt him a lot to have to give it up.

A bolt of lightning, directly overhead, startled the horse into a run. The rain came suddenly and heavily with almost constant lightning and thunder. We were drenched in seconds. Then the rain stopped as quickly as it had begun. The wagon sloshed through the puddles and the mud, and occasionally bogged down.

Then the sky lit up like the Fourth of July and the heavy rain came again.

We went through town quickly. Most of River Junction was dark except for the hotel and the depot. The town meeting was still going on. The depot doors were never locked, so the meetings would go on until the last two people left.

There was a slight opening through the clouds and the nearly full moon was reflected in the puddles in the road. The wind died down to a light, cool breeze. The rain had nearly stopped again.

As we neared home we could see the light from the parlor.

"We still have to put Mother's sewing machine together."

"You need to get to bed," said Dad. "Your mother will get suspicious if you stay up. I'll tell her I have some work to get done in the barn."

"Maybe we can work on it when I get home from school tomorrow," I suggested.

"No, I'll be helping Mr. Foster all afternoon," he said. "He helped with our planting today, so I'm helping him with his logging job."

I hopped down from the wagon and pulled the

barn doors open. It was just in time as another downpour hit.

"You go on in and get to bed. Tell your mother I'll be out here doing some work."

I waited for the rain to let up before I ran to the back door. When I went into the parlor, Mother was still working on her sewing. She had been taking in a lot of sewing and working very late into the evenings. With Christmas about two months away, she was trying to put away some extra money for gifts.

"Dad's got some things to do in the barn," I told her. "He said he'd be in later."

"Did you see the man in the Dobson house and apologize to him?"

"Yes, his name is Mr. Gehrmann. He's from San Francisco and you should see the clocks he—"

"Wait a minute," she interrupted me. "This sounds like a long story. Let's talk about it in the morning."

"OK. Good night."

I kissed her and went in to get ready for bed. I washed up and climbed under the covers. My body was so tired it ached and my mind churned with everything that had happened. I lay there trying to get to sleep. I was trying to *not* think of things that had happened that day. But that never seems to work.

I had almost forgotten to say my prayers. As I began to pray, Psalm 118:24 came to my mind. With all the problems of the day, there still were many things to "be glad" about.

What a day it had been.

But what a day Tuesday would be!

Chapter Ten

There I was standing in front of the whole class. Everyone was laughing at me because Miss Hartfield had hung a sign around my neck. The sign said simply, "The Cheater." Miss Hartfield handed Mary a big board and told her she could paddle me for looking at her test paper. Mary had that silly grin on her face and she was wearing a crown like a queen. She pulled back the board and swung as hard as she could.

"No!" I shouted.

"Mike," Dad was shaking me. "Wake up, Mike." I was still in bed.

"It sounded like you were having a bad dream," said Dad.

"Yeah," I tried to collect my thoughts. "I sure was."

"You were sure yelling."

"Did I wake you up?"

"No, your mother and I got up just a few minutes ago."

"What time is it?" I asked.

"It's almost time to get up, so you might as well get out of bed and get ready early. I'm going to take you to school before I go to help Mr. Foster. We can both talk to Miss Hartfield about this cheating incident."

"I didn't cheat!"

"I didn't mean it that way, Mike. I believe you."

He started out the door and then stopped and said, "How about starting the fires for us?"

"OK," I answered. "Hey, Dad, did you get it put together?"

"Almost," he whispered. "I think we can finish it this evening."

I said, "She'll sure be surprised when—"

"Shhhhh," he interrupted me as the door to Mother and Dad's room opened.

"What's going on in there?" she asked.

"I was having a bad dream and Dad woke me up."

"Well, let's all get dressed and we'll have breakfast."

"I'll get the stove fired up as soon as I get my clothes on, Mother."

Dad went out the back door to do his chores. I got dressed and gathered the wood for the fires. I built the fire in the stove and lit it. Then I stacked some kindling and logs in the fireplace. I took a wooden match from a can on the mantel and struck it on the hearth. The kindling crackled into flame. As the fire grew, the logs began to smoke and pop. Soon there was a roaring fire sending huge puffs of smoke up the chimney.

Mother came out of her room. She was dressed

and already had her hair up in big curls. She took her long, flowered apron off the hook and put it on. "That feels so good, Mike. Thank you for getting everything ready."

"You're welcome."

"Would you please check and see how many eggs you can find in the chicken coop?"

"Sure." I went outside and Dad was nowhere in sight. The light of dawn reflected off scattered clouds and lit the yard with a soft orange glow. A rumble of thunder told me the storm might not be finished.

As I entered the chicken coop, the rooster crowed at me. I gathered nine eggs from the nests. That was about the normal number on an average morning.

I went back into the barn to see if Dad was working on the surprise. Sure enough, he was up in the loft fitting some pieces together.

"Is that you, Mike?" he asked nervously.

"Yeah, I came out to get some eggs for Mother and I wanted to see if you had it put together yet."

"No, this is taking longer than I expected, but I think we can finish this evening."

Dad climbed down from the loft and began finishing his work in the barn.

"Do you think I could stop by Mr. Gehrmann's for a while after school today?"

"No, Mike. Remember your punishment."

"But maybe he needs help unpacking or something."

"No, Michael!" Dad said in his firm voice. "And don't ask me again."

I didn't say anything more. I went back into the house with the eggs. The smell of bacon was already filling the house and mother had the plates already set on that familiar checkered tablecloth.

"Here are the eggs."

"Thank you, Mike. Will you please ask your dad to come in for breakfast? It'll be ready in five minutes."

"Mother, do you think I should stop by Mr. Gehrmann's house today? Maybe I could help him unpack or put things away."

"No, Michael!" she answered firmly and changed the subject. "You may tell your dad to come in soon."

Dad was hitching the horse to the wagon. Bessie was the name I gave the horse when we got it. My parents tried to convince me that "Bessie" was a better name for a cow, but I liked the name. So it stuck. Bessie was a strong, beautiful chocolate-brown horse and looked nothing like a cow. Her mane and tail were black and shiny as coal.

"Dad," I called out, "Mother said breakfast will be ready in five minutes."

"OK, son. I'll be right in."

We sat down to a breakfast of bacon and eggs with biscuits and honey. I just loved biscuits with honey on them. In fact, I still do.

We talked mostly about our visit with Mr. Gehrmann and the story he had told us.

"He must have had a horrible accident," said Mother. "What kind of work does he do?"

"He didn't really say. In fact he seemed to avoid telling us," said Dad. "Whatever he did, he gave it up after the accident."

"But if he doesn't have a job of some kind, how can he afford to live?" I asked.

"Maybe he saved enough money from his job," said Mother.

"He must have had a job in a fancy building,"

said Dad, "because he talked about the big clock in the clock tower."

"Yeah, and he said something about not being able to face all those people," I added.

"If he had been ready to tell you, I'm sure he would have," said Mother. "His job must have been important to him and it probably hurt a lot to give it up."

"Well, whatever he did, he sure collected some beautiful clocks," said Dad.

"I wonder if he would have a nice clock for our mantel?" asked Mother.

"I could go see this afternoon!"

"No, Michael!" both Mother and Dad said together. They looked at each other and tried to keep from smiling. We all started laughing. We were all in a much better mood.

As Dad and I rode along in the wagon, I tried to think of how I would explain things to Miss Hart-field. If she didn't believe me or wouldn't listen, what good would telling the truth do? I was glad my dad was going along. He knew how I had stud-ied and how well I knew the states.

We passed the stables just as Charley was open-ing up. He waved to us.

"Hello, Charley," said Dad.

"Mornin' Mr. Roberts."

Dad stopped the wagon across from the depot and asked me, "Do you want to wait here for the other boys?"

"No."

"We could wait for a couple of minutes," said Dad.

"No, Dad, I don't want to see them this morn-ing."

"Did you boys have a fight?"

"No, it's just that they were making fun of me yesterday."

"OK, we can go on."

I didn't know about it yet, but a message was coming in to the telegraph office that would make this day different than any I had ever had.

Our wagon splashed through the puddles along Brooks Creek. For the first time in two years we could hear water running in the creek. I looked up at the sky—maybe more rain. The cool, fresh wind blew through the few leaves left on the trees, making them dance with a rustling noise. Some of them drifted to the ground, joining the others heaped along the roadside. No dust on the roads today, only mud and puddles. Hopefully a wet winter was on the way.

We passed Mr. Gehrmann's house. Smoke was already rising from the chimney. I yelled a hello to him, but I couldn't tell if he heard me from inside the house.

Just past Mr. Gehrmann's house, we passed the entrance to the old gold mine. It had been boarded up for many years but that didn't keep people out. A lot of us went in there even though the sign said, "Danger. Keep Out!"

The road climbed and turned and soon we came to the old bridge that crossed the gorge. Dad walked the horse over the bridge very slowly. He said he didn't trust that rickety old thing.

The water was rushing into the swimming hole and over the rocks below. It was dirty brown and full of dead logs and limbs. A big log thumped against one of the support beams and the bridge shook a little.

Across the bridge, we started into the pines

and cedars. Little streams of water ran down the hillsides and along the road. The ferns, bear clover, and other plants seemed to have come to life overnight.

We drove over the summit and down into the valley. The air was so clear and the view was spectacular. The sun felt warm against the back of my neck when it broke through the scattered clouds. The little town of Pine Ridge and the schoolhouse were clearly in view. As we drove closer and closer, I wondered what Miss Hartfield would say and do.

Thunder suddenly crackled, and I nearly fell out of the wagon.

Chapter Eleven

I laugh every time I think about Mr. Gehrmann and the boys telling how they first met.

Danny, Zach, and Freddy saw that I wasn't at the stables but they decided to wait for a few minutes. Then Charley came out of the blacksmith's shop wearing his leather apron. He was already sweaty from working over the coals.

"You boys waiting for Mike?"

"Yeah," they answered.

"He came by here just a few minutes ago with his father," said Charley. "They headed up Creek Road in their wagon."

"Thanks, Charley," said Zach. "Let's go."

"His pa is probably on his way to talk to Miss Hartfield about the cheating," said Danny.

"I bet he didn't do it," said Freddy.

"Sure he did," said Danny.

"What'll you bet?" asked Zach.

"A day's chores," said Danny.

"You're on," said Zach.

"Come on," said Freddy, "let's get going."

"Hey," said Danny, "let's see if we can get a look at that man at the Dobson house."

"I heard Pa say the man is an ugly sight," said Freddy.

"Last one there is a sissy!" yelled Zach.

They ran along Creek Road until the Dobson house was in view. As usual, Zach was first and Danny was last. They stopped behind the trunk of a huge oak tree. They watched to see if Mr. Gehrmann would come out. They didn't see him, so they sneaked up along the white picket fence. They still didn't see him. They crouched down and crept up to the side of the house and hid alongside the wagon. The horse had already been hitched to the wagon, so the boys expected "the man" to come out any second.

"Hey," whispered Danny. "I've got a great idea for a joke."

"What?" asked Zach.

"Let's tie this rope to the back of the wagon and around the outhouse," giggled Danny.

"Yeah," Zach started to giggle too, "and when he leaves—down it goes!"

"Shhhhhh." Danny and Zach covered their mouths to keep from being heard as they laughed.

"You better not!" said Freddy.

"Get the rope from the wagon," said Danny.

Zach peaked over the top of the wagon and quickly grabbed the rope. He ducked down behind the wagon again.

Freddy said, "I'm gettin' outa here." He sneaked away toward the road as Danny and Zach carried out their plan.

"What a chicken," they said as they sneaked to the back of the wagon. Zach tied the rope to the wagon and Danny walked the rope around the out-house. He had just finished tying the rope when the sound of a sneeze from inside the outhouse startled him.

"Ohhhhh!" Danny cried out. "Let's get out of here!"

"Hey, who's out there?" said Mr. Gehrmann.

Danny and Zach ran around the front of the wagon, past the house, through the trees, and *over* the picket fence. They were nearly shouting with nervous laughter as they ran up the road.

Mr. Gehrmann pushed the door, but it wouldn't budge. Through a crack in the door he watched the pranksters running away. He could also see the rope stretched to the back end of the wagon.

"Hey, come back here!" he shouted.

As he shouted, the horse moved and the wagon rolled slightly ahead. The rope pulled tight and the outhouse creaked as it did.

"Whoa," he tried to calm the horse as he thought about what could happen if it bolted.

He tried to push out a loose board, but the rope held it tightly in place. He looked out again and nobody was in sight. He started to call for help, but he was afraid to startle the horse again.

"Those stupid brats," he said to himself. "Wait 'til I get my hands on them!"

The wind grew stronger and the trees and leaves began to rustle. Again the horse moved and the wagon pulled the rope tighter.

"Whoa, boy, easy, easy."

He thought he might try to kick some boards out of the side of the little building. But he was afraid that too might startle the horse.

"Darn rascals!" he said in an angry tone of voice. But his anger soon faded as the memories of his childhood came to mind. He laughed to himself as he thought about some of the pranks he had pulled as a boy.

Again he peeked out. Through the trees and shrubs and past the picket fence he could see the road. Around the bend came a wagon. It was Miss Polly's little yellow wagon.

Chapter Twelve

Dad and I stepped down from the wagon and walked up to the schoolhouse. My heart was pounding in my head and I couldn't take a deep breath. I prayed silently, "Please help me, Lord." The front door was already open, so we went on in. Miss Hartfield was sitting at her desk looking through some papers. She didn't see us come in.

Dad cleared his throat to let her know we were there.

She looked up. "Oh, Mr. Roberts, I'm glad you came with Michael."

"Yes," he said. "I understand we have something to talk about."

"So I see you received my note," she said.

"We talked about this at home last night," he said. "We know that Michael had learned all of the states because we worked with him. I think he can explain what happened if he has a chance."

Dad put his arm around my shoulder and continued. "Michael is a good boy and I believe him when he says he didn't cheat."

My face turned warm and I was sure I was blushing.

Miss Hartfield grinned at me and nodded. Then she took a deep breath and her expression sobered. She stood up, walked around her desk, and stood looking out the window.

"I'm sorry about not listening to Mike," she began to apologize. "I've been upset lately."

She stopped for a moment but still looked out the window toward the pine-covered mountains. "You see, my father's been quite sick. I've been very concerned about him and my temper's been very short."

"I'm sorry to hear about your father," said Dad.

She walked back over to her desk and stood behind it. She wiped her eyes and cleared her throat. "When I graded the tests last night, I knew I'd made a mistake in blaming Mike."

"How?" asked Dad.

"Mike got a hundred percent."

"Wouldn't that be possible if he cheated?" asked Dad.

"Yes, but you see," she said, "Mary got two of the states wrong."

Miss Hartfield stopped for a moment to look through the papers on her desk. I thought about what Mary had said about Indiana and Illinois. Could it be that Mary made that mistake? I gritted my teeth to keep from smiling.

"Mary missed Indiana and Illinois," she said, "but that isn't what convinced me."

"What did?" asked Dad.

She hesitated, grinned, and said, "What convinced me was Mike's horrible spelling. He spelled so many wrong that it was obvious he hadn't copied. Mary is a perfect speller and she spelled all of the states correctly."

For once in my life, I was happy to be a poor speller. I was even happy to admit that Mary was a good one.

Miss Hartfield said, "Mike, I'm sorry."

"Oh, that's alright." I took a deep breath and my heart calmed to a normal pace. "Thank you, Lord," I whispered.

"Well, Mike, I need to get going," said Dad. "Mr. Foster is probably chopping down trees already."

"Thanks for coming, Mr. Roberts," said Miss Hartfield. "I'm sorry—"

Dad interrupted, "Don't worry about it. It was an understandable mistake."

He added, "We'll be praying for your father."

"Thank you."

"Bye, Dad."

"Mike, school won't start for quite a while," said Miss Hartfield. "You may go out and play if you like."

"Is there anything I can help you with?"

"No, thanks, Mike." she said, "I have everything ready for class today." I sensed that she wanted to be by herself.

I walked out the front door. A group of students were already gathered on the steps. Joey, Louisa, and Mary were there. Louisa didn't even look at me. It seemed as though she was trying to ignore me. Mary didn't ignore me. She looked up with that silly grin. "Cheater," Mary said, with a nasty whine in her voice. And then she stuck out her tongue. I just grinned back at her and walked on. I felt so good inside. Smart-aleck Mary was finally going to be put in her place. I could hardly wait to see the expression on her face when she saw her paper.

I guess it must've been about this time that Miss Polly and Mrs. Collins were pulling up to the front gate of the Dobson house.

Chapter Thirteen

For many years Emily Collins told the story of what happened that day. Each time she told it she laughed about it.

"He's home," Miss Polly remarked to Emily. "There's a fire in the fireplace and his horse and wagon are here."

The ladies got out of the wagon and Miss Polly tied the horse to the fence and got her basket from behind the seat. She and Emily walked through the gate and up the walkway.

"This place is sure run-down," Polly whispered.

"From what I hear, I think he's quite wealthy," said Emily. "So why would he want to buy this old place?"

"I don't know," answered Polly. "It's rather far out of town. Perhaps he wants privacy."

They walked onto the porch and Miss Polly knocked on the door. "Remember," she whispered, "be prepared when you see his face."

There was no answer.

"Hello?" Miss Polly knocked again.

Three times she knocked and there was still no answer. Emily looked into the parlor window. She didn't see anyone inside. Then she looked around the corner of the house and said, "He must be around here someplace."

"Is there anyone home?" Miss Polly hollered.

"Yes," came a muffled voice. "I'm in here."

The women looked at each other and grinned as they realized where he was. They turned and headed back toward the front porch to wait for him to return to the house.

"Help me," said the muffled voice.

They looked at each other again. "Help me?" they asked each other. They walked past the horse and wagon toward the outhouse.

"What's wrong?" asked Miss Polly.

"Are you ill?" asked Emily.

"I'm trapped in here," he answered. "Help me out."

As they walked closer they could see the rope leading from the wagon to the outhouse.

"Be careful," said Mr. Gehrmann. "Whatever you do, don't spook the horse."

They untied the rope from the wagon and then the outhouse and out came Mr. Gehrmann. Miss Polly and Emily both tried very hard to keep straight faces.

"Go ahead and laugh," he said.

They did.

"I'm Polly Porter."

"Yes, I remember. I'm Ed Gehrmann."

"And this is Emily Collins," said Polly.

"How do you do?" Emily didn't seem surprised

when she first saw his face. As a newspaper reporter she had seen scars like that before and she could tell what had happened to him.

"I guess I'm much better, *now*," he said.

"Who did this to you?" Emily asked.

"Some young boys came around earlier this morning and tied that rope around the outhouse when I was . . . uh . . . in it," he said. "It was so windy I didn't even hear them. When I sneezed I guess I startled one of the boys and they ran away."

"Do you know who they were?" asked Emily.

"I think they're friends of Mike's," he said.

"You mean Mike Roberts?" asked Polly. "Do you know him?"

"Yes," he said. "We had an interesting meeting yesterday." He looked at Miss Polly and continued, "In fact, I had *two* interesting meetings with people yesterday."

"Well, I'm glad we came when we did," Miss Polly spoke up to change the subject. "Oh, we brought your 'Welcome Wagon' package too."

"Well, thank you. Let's go in and sit down."

They entered through the back door. The kitchen was still cluttered with many unopened boxes and crates. The smell of coffee and fresh paint combined to make an unusual odor. Mr. Gehrmann asked if they would like something to drink.

"No, thank you," they said.

"What can I do to thank you ladies?"

"Oh, nothing," said Polly.

"How about a story for the paper?" asked Emily.

"The paper?" he asked.

"Yes, I'm a reporter," said Emily, "for the *River Junction Expositor*. It comes out every week."

"I don't think I have a story for you," he said.

"You know," said Emily, "they had quite a discussion about you at the depot last night."

"At the depot?"

"Well, you see," said Polly, "the men all get together and discuss things down at the depot."

"And why was I the point of discussion last night?"

"My husband said they were wondering about you sneaking into town without anyone knowing why," said Emily. "The old-timers of the town are rather suspicious of strangers around here."

Miss Polly added, "Mr. Albright is coming out here this afternoon to talk to you."

"I didn't *sneak* into town," he said, "and Mr. Albright knows that. Why's he coming out here?"

"To tell you that the townspeople are concerned," answered Emily.

"Maybe I should just leave if my being here is going to cause a big problem."

"Perhaps if you told everyone about yourself," said Emily, "it just might ease the tension."

"Mrs. Collins, I think you can easily understand why I want my privacy," said Mr. Gehrmann. "Someone told me that River Junction was a great place to live. Maybe that person was wrong. It sounds as though the people have already decided that I'm not welcome here."

"It may sound that way," said Emily, "but it's nothing personal. The people of River Junction just want to know about the people who come here. It seems as though all of our troubles have come from outsiders. The people of this town are very close, and they want to keep it that way."

"And you did come rather secretively," added Polly.

"Well, I can understand how you feel, I guess," he said.

"Wouldn't it be easier to meet the people through a newspaper story than to face them?" asked Emily.

He stopped and thought for a moment, and then asked, "If I tell you about myself, will you let me read the story and approve it before you print it?"

"Of course," said Emily. "When can we start?"

Mr. Gehrmann stood up and walked around the kitchen. He looked back at Miss Polly and Emily. They both sat still and breathless, waiting for him to speak. He sat back down at the table and asked the two to make themselves comfortable.

They smiled, sighed, and leaned forward in their chairs. Then he began to tell them his story.

Chapter Fourteen

About the time Mr. Gehrmann was telling his story I was sitting by myself under the huge oak tree. Miss Hartfield came out to ring the final bell and everyone headed for the school building. A few of the students made some comments about the cheating. I just ignored them and walked faster toward the front steps. There were a few odd glances from other students. I was so anxious to have everyone find out that I hadn't cheated. We filed into the coatroom and put our things away. I noticed that my three buddies weren't at school yet.

We stood by our desks, ready for the flag salute. The door banged open and in ran Freddy. Zach and Danny were right behind him. Miss Hartfield made a comment about being on time for class. Joey led the flag salute. When we came to the end of the salute, Mary stuck her nose in the air, looked at me, and said, ". . . and *justice* for all."

I smiled at her and gave her a wink. She looked away and then I noticed that Danny had seen me wink at her. I thought, "Why did I do that?"

"I'm sure you're anxious to find out how you did on the test yesterday," said Miss Hartfield.

There was a murmur of excited voices and the nodding of heads. Some of the class turned to look at me, but I just kept my eyes focused straight ahead. Miss Hartfield tapped her ruler on the desk to get everyone's attention. Heads turned toward the front of the room and the class was silent.

"We have five students with scores of one-hundred percent," she said. "I'll call out the names and those people can come up and get their papers."

There was a little noise again as some students squirmed in their desks. Mary sat on the edge of her seat waiting to jump up and get her paper. Miss Hartfield shuffled through the papers on her desk and pulled out the five best.

She cleared her throat and began announcing the names, "Harriet Burns." She waited for Harriet to get to the front of the classroom.

"Katie Daniels," then she paused again.

"John Groves."

"Louisa Foster."

Before she could announce the last name, Mary was out of her seat and headed for the front of the classroom. Miss Hartfield finally said the last name, "And Michael Roberts."

Mary took a few steps backwards and slumped into her seat. She had a look of disbelief on her red face. The classroom filled with murmurs again. As I walked by Danny's desk, I heard Zach ask him, "When do I collect?" There was even more satisfaction in knowing that Danny had lost a bet on whether or not I had cheated. It made me feel good to know that Zach trusted me.

"Let's have a hand for these students," said Miss Hartfield, and the class broke into applause. Except for Mary. As the class clapped and cheered I noticed two men standing in the back of the room. They were Cliff Brooks and Mr. Fisher. Miss Hartfield noticed them too. She asked us to sit down. The class quieted down and one by one they turned to see who was there.

We were surprised to see Cliff so far from the depot. Mr. Fisher was the teacher of the upper-grade students and we seldom saw him downstairs. Cliff was holding a golden-colored envelope and Mr. Fisher had the golden-colored telegram from inside it.

"May I talk with you, Miss Hartfield?" asked Mr. Fisher.

"Surely," she said. She walked to the back of the room. As she walked closer to Mr. Fisher, she seemed to realize what was happening. Her smile slowly changed to a frown.

"Let's talk out here," said Mr. Fisher. They disappeared into the coatroom and the class sat quietly hoping to hear what was going on.

We heard the front door close. Then, through the window, we could see Cliff walking Miss Hartfield to her wagon. She was covering her face and walking slowly while holding Cliff by the arm. He helped her into the wagon and got in the seat to drive.

The classroom suddenly filled with chatter as the students wondered what was happening. A few students ran to the window to watch Miss Hartfield and Cliff leave.

Mr. Fisher came into the room and commanded in his big, strong voice, "Sit down and be quiet." He didn't have to say it twice. The class returned to order and everyone sat in silence.

He walked to the front of the classroom and began to explain, "Miss Hartfield just received some bad news. Her father died early this morning."

He waited for the talking to stop again; then he continued, "She will be going home to be with her family and she probably won't be back until Monday."

Someone asked, "Are you going to be our teacher?"

"No, that won't be possible," he answered. "I'll try to make arrangements for some of my oldest students to be here tomorrow to help you with your studies."

The classroom was noisy again. But there was a lot more groaning than talking. Most of us usually acted as though we didn't like Miss Hartfield, but we really did. We didn't want someone else taking over her job.

"Well, I guess there's nothing more we can do today," said Mr. Fisher. "Get your things together and you may be excused to go home."

That kind of an announcement would usually bring a big cheer from a classroom full of students, but we were unhappy to hear the bad news about Mr. Hartfield. Except for Danny, everyone left the classroom as though we were walking out of church. Danny was smiling as he thought about getting out of school early.

Katie Daniels punched him in the shoulder and said, "Stop that! Don't you have any feelings?"

He tried to laugh it off, but he could see that no one was laughing at him or with him. He looked down at his feet and shuffled out of the room as quietly as the rest of us. Mr. Fisher closed the door. The key clicked and he shook the door to make sure it was locked.

Chapter Fifteen

Mr. Fisher climbed the staircase at the side of the building. We could hear him call out to the older students, "Let's get back to work!"

We walked slowly down the schoolhouse steps and across the schoolyard without anyone saying a thing. Some of the girls were crying and most of the boys were trying to pretend they had no feelings at all. I couldn't help thinking about my grandfather. He died just a couple of years before. I felt sorry for Miss Hartfield because I remember how my mother cried and cried for a long time. Our bad news also came in a telegram. The doctor in the San Francisco hospital sent it to the depot and Mr. Hawkins delivered it himself. I had many dreams about telegrams bringing bad news. It was almost a year before the nightmares stopped.

Freddy and Zach were waiting for Danny and me on the road in front of the school.

"Well, Danny," said Freddy, "I guess you owe Mike an apology."

"Yeah," added Zach, "and you owe me a day's worth of chores!"

Looking down at his feet and speaking softly, Danny said, "Sorry, Mike."

"Thanks," I said. We walked up the road toward the summit and never talked about it again.

From inside the woods came the muffled thuds of axes cutting into trees. A voice shouted, "Timber!" There was a squeaking crackle as the tree began its fall and the final booming rumble as it hit the ground. I wondered if Dad had chopped that one down. It was difficult to tell where the tree had fallen until a cloud of dust rose to mark the spot.

The weather had changed so much since morning. The clouds were thick over the summit and completely blocked out the sun.

"Let's go work on the swimming hole," said Danny.

"I can't," I said. "I got into trouble, so my folks said to come straight home after school." I really was planning on going into town to talk to some of the people about jobs. I knew Dad would be up in the mountains with Mr. Foster. I just hoped the stormy weather would keep Mother at home. If she saw me in town, I would be in much more trouble than I was already.

"Ah, come on, Mike," said Danny. "They'll never know if you stay just a little while."

"And we can get done a lot faster," added Zach.

"Oh, alright," I gave in. I didn't want to tell them what I really had in mind. Dad never wanted anyone to know we were poor and struggling. Money problems, he said, were something we were never to discuss outside our home.

"Hey, Mike," said Freddy, "will you tell us what happened at the Dobson house yesterday?"

"Before or after you chickened out?" I asked in a joking way.

Freddy spoke right up as though he hadn't heard my comment. "Is it true that he looks like some kind of monster?"

"Who told you that?" I asked.

"My pa was at the depot last night and they were talking about the stranger."

"Yeah," said Zach, "someone said something about him attacking Miss Polly."

"That's not true," I snapped. "He didn't hurt her. He's a good man!"

While we walked toward the swimming hole I answered their questions about what had happened. They told me the men at the depot were suspicious about the way this stranger had come into town. I told them about going to his house to apologize to him. Then I told them the story he had told us.

When we reached the bridge we began to plan how we would make the dam under the bridge and deepen the swimming hole. The water was rushing under the bridge. It was so loud we had to shout to hear one another. Logs and other debris were building up behind the bridge and the water was already rising.

"Let's roll some big boulders off the edge of the bridge so that they'll pile up behind those beams," suggested Zach.

"Boy, the way this water is flowing," said Freddy, "it will fill this swimming hole right away."

We did the work from above because the rushing water had washed out our only path. The deep gorge was too steep and the water was moving too fast for us to go down under the bridge.

"We need to build a ladder," I said, "so we can climb up onto the bridge from the swimming hole."

"Here's a good boulder over here, Mike," said Freddy. "Give me a hand!" The rock was too large to carry, so we rolled it to the edge of the cliff and pushed it over. It rolled down the steep bank and onto the pile of debris.

Danny and Zach pushed a big boulder onto the bridge and tried to slide it to the edge. With a grunt and the count of "One, two, three," they managed to push it over. It splashed into the water and, with a "thunk," fell against one of the pilings of the bridge. The wood popped and the bridge shook a little.

"Hey, be careful!" shouted Freddy.

"Yeah," I added, "this bridge is old and weak."

"Don't get excited," said Danny. "When we get this dam built, it'll make the bridge even stronger."

"Look at that!" shouted Zach. He pointed to a tree floating sideways down the river. It looked like a whole tree that had been uprooted by the storm. It bumped against the pilings at the foot of the bridge and remained jammed into place by the force of the rushing water.

"How's that for a ready-made dam?" asked Zach.

"All we need to do is make it stronger now," said Danny. "Let's get some more boulders and some limbs and branches too."

The bridge creaked as the tree snuggled tighter against it. More and more logs and debris gathered behind it. The water level was rising rapidly.

Danny and Zach continued tossing and rolling rocks and boulders into the water. Freddy went up the road to gather branches. I decided to see what loose wood I could find down the road toward the mine.

I returned with an armload of sticks and branches. I felt like a beaver I once saw rebuilding its home. Freddy had returned and was helping the other two move a big boulder into place.

"Hurry, Mike," shouted Danny. "We need a hand here."

I was just a few yards from the bridge when one of the pilings under the bridge gave way. The bridge slumped slightly. Freddy ran to the other end of the bridge and shouted, "Get off! It's going to collapse!"

Before he could reach the road on the other side, some other pilings crumbled. The debris and water that had been trapped behind the bridge rushed under it and pulled down the other pilings. The bridge collapsed with the worst noise I ever heard.

Freddy had jumped to a ledge on the other side of the gorge. I just stood there feeling completely helpless. I thought for sure Danny and Zach had drowned or been crushed by the falling bridge.

A huge section from the center of the bridge floated on the churning mass of water. I couldn't believe it! There was Zach! He was lying on his stomach on the section as it floated along like a raft.

I shouted across the gorge to Freddy. "Are you alright?"

"My leg, I think it's broken!"

"I'll go for help," I told him. "Don't try to move."

I ran along the edge of the bank. I could hear a shout for help. It was Danny! He was just a few feet from Zach. Zach reached out and tried to grab him but they drifted apart as the rushing water took them farther downstream. I kept running along the bank, hoping there would be some place I could help them.

Danny disappeared under the water.

"Oh, God, help him!" I knew Danny couldn't swim very well.

With the next try, Zach reached out and grabbed Danny by the arm. Danny struggled and finally climbed on board.

The section of bridge wedged in the rocks and debris near the center of the river while the water rushed by them on both sides. Even though their raft seemed somewhat secure, they looked scared.

"Hang on!" I shouted. "And I'll go for help."

I took off running and climbing uphill toward the road. I didn't even think about where I was going. I just went. Then I remembered Mr. Gehrmann. His house was the closest. I would go there.

I scrambled up the hillside through the manzanita bushes. It was a steep climb and I slipped a few times. I reached the road and began running toward Mr. Gehrmann's house. I ran as fast as I could.

My legs and chest began to ache, but I ran on and on. My throat burned as it dried out. When I reached the old mine I knew I didn't have far to go and that gave me an extra boost of energy. My legs seemed to be getting heavier and heavier.

The first thing I saw as I came around the bend in the road was Miss Polly's yellow wagon.

I began yelling, "Mr. Gehrmann, Miss Polly, help!"

I ran through the gate. The door opened and out came Mr. Gehrmann. Right behind him were Miss Polly and Mrs. Collins.

"What's wrong, Mike?" he asked.

"Zach and Danny need help . . . the bridge collapsed!" I swallowed and caught my breath. "They're stuck in the middle of the river!"

"Come on, Mike. Let's get into the wagon," he said. "You ladies head into town and send more help."

We ran to the wagon and he yelled further instructions to the two ladies. "Tell them to bring ropes, blankets, and medical supplies. Hurry!"

He slapped the horse with the reins. "Yah, git up!"

We headed up the road at full speed.

The little yellow wagon headed in the opposite direction, toward town.

Chapter Sixteen

A few pilings in the water and some boards hanging from the edge of the gorge were all that was left of the bridge. Freddy was still stuck on the ledge about 10 feet below where the bridge had been. The water was rushing by a few feet below him. He tried to reach a rock and pull himself up. The rock gave way and he was showered with rocks and mud.

"God, if you're really here, I need your help." Freddy told me that was his first real attempt at prayer. "Please help me!" His leg was throbbing with pain. He pulled up the left leg of his pants to see what was wrong. There was a huge gash with the splinter of a bone sticking out of it. When he saw the wound, it seemed to make it hurt even more. He ripped a piece of cloth from his torn shirt and tied it around the bleeding wound.

"Help!" he shouted. There was nobody around to hear.

He tried again. "Is there anybody there?"

He wondered if Danny and Zach were still alive and if they were nearby. "Danny . . . Zach!" There was no answer.

He began to feel weak and dizzy, so he put his head back and closed his eyes.

Danny and Zach, several yards downstream, were rocked and jolted by the surging water. They still clung to the bridge section. The dirty, reddish-brown floodwater carried more and more debris past them.

"Look out!" shouted Danny as a snake slithered onto the boards. They thought it was a rattlesnake but they didn't wait to find out. Zach kicked it into the water. They watched as more snakes floated past. Occasionally they would see one clinging to a branch that went floating by them. Other animals went by in the water. Some were swimming; others were floating lifelessly.

Another surge of water pushed the boards off the rocks and they were drifting downstream again. The river turned and dropped over some more rocks. The smashing of the boards against the rocks nearly knocked the boys loose a couple of times, but they managed to hold on.

Again they jammed against a group of rocks and they were stuck. Another chance to hope for rescue.

"Help!" Zach shouted. "Somebody, please, help!"

"I don't think anyone can hear us," said Danny. He talked loudly over the roar of the river. "We've drifted away from the road."

"That rumbling sound ahead of us," Zach cried out, "that's Thunder Falls. We're only a few hundred feet from them."

"We've got to keep from floating any farther," said Danny, "or we'll be washed over the falls!"

Our parents had always told us to stay away from the falls. Anything going over the falls would be smashed against the bed of rocks below and held under by the tumbling water.

"Here, take some of these boards." Danny pulled a few boards from the edge of their raft. He continued his instructions to Zach. "Try to jam them in between the rocks. Let's see if we can keep this thing from moving again."

The muddy water swirled around and over them. Occasionally they would be splashed in the face by a big wave. They worked hard with the little energy they had left wedging boards against the rocks. Feeling secure again, they rested and waited for help.

"I just noticed, I'm cold," said Danny.

"Me too," Zach answered as his body shivered.

"Mike should be back any time now with some help."

Zach looked all around and back upstream. "I wonder what happened to Freddy."

"I don't know. I never saw him after he yelled that the bridge was collapsing."

"I saw him running," said Zach, "and the next thing I knew, the bridge was going down."

"And all I remember," commented Danny, "is falling off the bridge as it dropped and tipped. I fell into the water and it kept pushing me under. I thought I was going to drown." He smiled and looked at Zach, "I was sure glad to see you when I came up the last time."

Zach smiled and nodded.

The boards shifted under the pressure of the rushing water and they grabbed on tightly!

Chapter Seventeen

"Git up!" Mr. Gehrmann shouted orders to his horse. The wagon bounced violently over the ruts and through the puddles. I nearly fell backwards over the seat. We sped along the road past the old mine.

He shouted over the loud clattering of the wagon. "What happened, Mike?"

"The bridge collapsed with Danny, Zach, and Freddy on it. Freddy jumped and made it to a ledge on the other side of the gorge."

"Is he alright?"

"I think he has a broken leg, but he seemed alright."

"What about the other two?"

"Danny and Zach were floating on a piece of the bridge and it got stuck on some rocks. But they're clear out in the middle of the river."

"Where?"

"Just a little bit farther." I looked for the spot but the landscape looked different going in the other direction. "Here, stop here!"

Mr. Gehrmann pulled tight on the reins, shouted out a healthy "whoa," and stepped on the brake handle. The back wheel locked and the wagon skidded to a stop on the gravel shoulder of the road.

"Is this the place, Mike?"

"I'm almost positive it is."

"Let's go," he said. "Grab those ropes from the wagon."

We slid down the steep hillside on the seats of our pants until we reached level ground. I ran over to the edge of the gorge where I had seen them last. "They're gone!"

"Don't worry, Mike. Maybe you just picked the wrong spot."

"No, I'm sure this is where they were."

"Let's head downstream," he said. "What's the river like below here?"

"There are lots of rocks and rapids." I had a horrible feeling as I thought about what else was there. "And Thunder Falls!"

"A waterfall?"

"Yes." I got panicky. "We've got to get them before they get to the falls!"

"Is there a road that comes out above the falls?"

"No," I answered, "but the wagon could make it."

"Can you handle it?"

"Sure!" I was pleased he would trust me with his horse and wagon.

"Can I get to the falls on foot?" he asked.

"Yeah, if you take that path." I pointed to an opening through the brush.

"OK," he said. "You go up and get the wagon and meet me above the falls. I'll go on foot."

"Wouldn't it be faster if I just rode the horse down there?" I asked.

"If they're hurt, we'll need the wagon to carry them back to the road. My horse's name is Samson. He'll do anything you ask if you're firm with him."

I asked, "Do you want any of the ropes?"

"I'll take that extra long one," he answered. "You take the others, tie them to the wagon, and be ready to throw them if they're needed."

I ran to the foot of the hill and started my second climb up that steep slope to the road above.

Mr. Gehrmann called to me. "What did you say their names are?"

"Danny and Zach."

"OK. Let's get going." Mr. Gehrmann headed through the bushes as I continued my climb. I could hear him in the distance calling, "Danny . . . Zach . . . Danny . . ."

Breathlessly, I prayed, "Keep them safe until we get to them."

Chapter Eighteen

While Mr. Gehrmann and I were trying to find
the boys, Miss Polly's little yellow wagon swerved
around the curve in the road and bounced across
the railroad track. Miss Polly and Emily were anx-
iously looking for someone who could help Mr.
Gehrmann. The wagon slid around the corner to
the right and headed for the sheriff's office. All the
while, Miss Polly was shouting, "Help! We need
help!"

Mr. Hawkins and Andy Brooks were the first to
appear on the street. They went running across
the street from the depot to the sheriff's office.
Sheriff Goodwin soon came out of his office. He
was still putting on his holster as he came out.

"What's going on?" His voice was always so
calm.

Miss Polly and Emily both started talking at
once. Then Miss Polly stopped and let Emily

explain. "The bridge collapsed. Michael said Zach and Danny need help."

"Where are they?" he asked.

"Mike just said they were stuck in the middle of the river," said Emily. "He and Mr. Gehrmann went to help."

"Isn't Gehrmann that fellow who bought the Dobson place?" asked Sheriff Goodwin.

"Yes," said Emily. "He told us to bring more ropes, some blankets, and medical supplies."

"We have to hurry!" said Miss Polly.

The sheriff began giving orders to people in the growing crowd. "Andy, get some ropes and blankets. Dave, is that your wagon? Let's get it loaded." He didn't give anyone a chance to say anything. He just continued spouting out orders. "Polly, run over and get Doctor Powell. I just saw him at the hotel a few minutes ago. Emily, you set up the doc's office. We'll bring the boys back there."

The crowd broke up and everyone scattered in a dozen different directions. Mrs. Baxter came out of the General Store just as the crowd was breaking up. She asked what was going on and some of the people told her the story.

She asked if Freddy was with the other boys and no one knew for sure. "Oh, no, it can't be!" she said, almost crying. "They're supposed to be in school." She looked around frantically. "Can someone give me a ride up there?"

Mr. Harris came over to Mrs. Baxter and took her into the lobby of the hotel. "It won't do any good for you to go up there," he told her. "Wait here and we'll get the news to you as soon as we hear something."

The first wagon left with Dave Logan driving and Andy Brooks riding along.

Sheriff Goodwin sent out his deputies to get the Alexanders and Mr. Baxter. Then Mr. Hawkins took one of the horses tied up outside the hotel and rode off to tell Mr. and Mrs. Malone. Danny's house was just south of town.

The sheriff mounted his horse and headed out of town. The street in front of the depot was humming with activity. A few men jumped on their horses and followed the sheriff past the depot and across the tracks.

Emily dashed through the door and into Doctor Powell's office. That was nothing unusual around the Powell's house. The door was always open, 24 hours a day. It wasn't really an office. It was just the parlor of their house that was set up with a couple of cots and cabinets full of medical supplies. The walls were covered with all sorts of charts: eye charts, skeletal charts, and diagrams of different parts of the body. The shelves were crammed full of medical books and journals. Above his desk hung degrees from some eastern college.

"Mrs. Powell!"

Mrs. Powell came through the swinging door that led to the kitchen. "What is it, Emily?"

"There's been an accident," said Emily. "We need to get the office ready for when they bring in the boys."

"What boys? What happened?"

"Mike Roberts was up at the bridge. He said it collapsed with Danny and Zach on it."

"Let's get out bandages and medicines," said Mrs. Powell. "I'll boil some water to sterilize Doc's instruments. You can get a couple more cots from the closet and set them up over there by the window. There may be more people hurt."

They were soon joined by Miss Polly and the three of them had the place ready in a few minutes. The door opened again and in came Mr. and Mrs. Malone.

"Where's Danny?" Mrs. Malone looked around as though she thought he was already there.

Polly told her, "The doctor will be here in a minute. The sheriff and some of the men have gone out to help Mr. Gehrmann get the boys."

"Who's Mr. Gehrmann?"

"He's that stranger living in the Dobson house," answered Mr. Malone.

"Don't you fret," said Miss Polly. "Everybody's doing what they can. Danny is going to be alright."

"Why weren't they in school?" asked Mrs. Malone.

"Mr. Hawkins said school was let out early because Miss Hartfield's father passed on and she had to leave to go home," explained Polly.

The busy activity continued at the Powell's house. Soon Mr. and Mrs. Alexander arrived. The parents comforted each other as Miss Polly and Emily told them all they knew. There was a large group of interested friends waiting outside on the porch.

Inside Doctor Powell's office, the waiting parents sat silently on the cots as Miss Polly and Emily stood by the windows watching for the first signs of a wagon heading back into town. There was an unusual silence as though the entire town was holding its breath.

Chapter Nineteen

I climbed into the wagon and untied the reins from the brake handle. I pulled tight on the right rein and ordered, "Come on, Samson!" He stepped out and pulled the big wagon around in the road with almost no effort at all. I drove him as hard as he would go. As he galloped at top speed, the wagon bounced along behind. I bounced clear off the seat a couple of times as we went over some rocky bumps.

Samson managed to put his big hooves directly into the mud puddles whenever he got a chance. I was showered with muddy water. By that time my school clothes were beyond help. Where they weren't torn they were covered with mud and dirt. But I knew Mother would be more understanding that day than she had been the day before about my ruining my clothes.

Just past the old mine entrance I slowed Samson to a walk. The clearing to the right led to the river just above the falls. There was a steep slope most of the way and I was afraid of Samson getting away from me. I put my foot on the brake handle and pushed. I held the reins even tighter and braced my other leg against the front of the wagon.

"Easy, boy," I continued to remind him.

We reached the edge of the river and I turned the big horse and wagon around to face uphill. The back of the wagon was only a few feet from the rushing water. I locked the brake handle into position and jumped down with the reins still in my hand.

"Whoa, Samson," I said firmly. "Take it easy, boy."

He stood leaning forward with some effort. It was as though he knew he had to hold the wagon in place. He reminded me of the horses at the rodeo pulling tight on the rope after the rider has lassoed a calf. I grabbed some rocks and put them behind the wheels. When the wagon finally seemed secure to me I began to look around. There was no sign of either Danny or Zach.

The ground almost shook and gray mist filled the air as the water rumbled and plummeted over the falls. Logs, limbs, and pieces of the old fallen bridge tossed about in the rapids. I had a horrible feeling that Danny and Zach had already gone over the falls. But I tried to put that thought out of my mind.

I got the ropes out and began tying them on the wagon as Mr. Gehrmann had told me. I watched Samson closely and kept reminding him, "Whoa, boy, take it easy." When the wagon and ropes were in place I started looking for Danny and Zach again.

Mr. Gehrmann kept calling Danny and Zach as he continued down the path. The boys were nearby, but they couldn't hear him over the roar of the river.

"I wonder what happened to Mike," Danny said to Zach.

"I hope he brings help soon," said Zach. "I can't . . ."

"Look!" Danny interrupted Zach with a shout. "There's somebody up there!"

Mr. Gehrmann spotted the boys just as they saw him. They waved their arms to make sure he saw them. He waved back.

"Don't move," he hollered. "I'll try to get down a little closer." They couldn't understand what he said, but they could tell he was there to help.

Mr. Gehrmann climbed over some rocks and slid down the bank. He caught himself on the low-hanging branch of an oak tree just short of going into the water himself.

I hadn't gone very far before I saw Mr. Gehrmann tying a rope around the huge oak tree at the edge of the river. Then I saw Danny and Zach. I ran to help.

As I ran closer, I could hear Mr. Gehrmann shouting instructions to Danny and Zach. "One of you boys tie this rope around your waist. Leave enough rope for the other one to tie around his waist too."

He threw the rope and Danny caught it.

"Mr. Gehrmann!"

"Mike, come and help!"

When I reached Mr. Gehrmann, Danny and Zach had the rope tied around them.

"OK. Try to climb over to these rocks." Mr. Gehrmann's voice was strong and reassuring as he pointed to some rocks closer to the river bank. "Mike and I will pull the rope in."

Danny and Zach stood on their hands and knees on what was left of the bridge. Danny was the first one to reach for the rocks nearby. The rocks were slippery and Danny couldn't find a place to hold on.

"Pull the rope tighter," he shouted.

We did and he lunged forward and grabbed the top of a large rock. The river water poured over him, but he was able to hang on. Zach followed him. He managed to take hold of a log that was caught in the rocks.

Danny started to move for the next bunch of rocks. As he did, he slipped. He fell into the rushing water and Zach was pulled in with him. The rope snapped tight and pulled through our hands. I looked down and blood oozed out of my fist.

"Pull harder, Mike," Mr. Gehrmann shouted. I gritted my teeth, trying to forget my sore, raw hands, and pulled. The force of the water seemed impossible to overcome, but we kept pulling. Danny and Zach grabbed and kicked and swam and gasped for air. With the last bits of energy the four of us had, the boys safely made it out of the swift current.

There on the muddy bank of the river the four of us lay. We didn't move except for making the effort to breathe.

Danny finally caught enough breath to say, "Thanks."

"I thought you were drowned. It's a good thing I found Mr. Gehrmann."

They both said, "Thanks, Mr. Gehrmann."

"I'm just glad I was around to help," said Mr. Gehrmann. "If it had been earlier in the morning I might have been *tied up*."

"We're sorry, Mr. Gehrmann," said Zach. I couldn't understand why Zach would be apologizing.

"Don't worry about it," he said. "Do you boys remember this rope?" He gave them a big grin. All three of them broke into laughter. I still didn't know what they were talking about or what they were laughing about, but I felt like laughing too. All of us were laughing and didn't even notice Andy and Dave coming up behind us.

"It sounds like everyone is alright," said Andy.

"I think we're all just very tired and sore," said Mr. Gehrmann. He started to stick out his hand to shake Andy's but he noticed how bloody and dirty it was. "I'm Ed Gehrmann."

"I'm Andy Brooks."

"How did you find us?" Mr. Gehrmann asked.

"Dave and I spotted the wagon from the road."

"Freddy!" I suddenly remembered. "We've got to help him."

"Where is he?" asked Dave.

"He was stuck on a ledge when the bridge collapsed," I told them. "He's on the other side of the gorge just below where the bridge was."

"Dave, you get these boys into that wagon and take them to Doc Powell's house," ordered Andy. "Ed and I will take your wagon and get Freddy."

Sheriff Goodwin had already ridden out to where Freddy was. Freddy had passed out and didn't answer when the sheriff called to him. Other men arrived on horseback and began rigging ropes so that the sheriff could cross the river and get Freddy.

They threw one rope across and tried to lasso

part of a broken piling. They missed a few times. Finally the rope fell over the top of the wooden stub and was pulling tight.

Sheriff Goodwin tied a rope around his waist and started out over the rushing water. He hung onto the tight rope by his feet and hands like a possum in a tree. He worked his way across and reached the ledge where Freddy was trapped. He felt for Freddy's pulse and shouted back to the others, "He's alive!"

Andy, Mr. Gehrmann and I arrived just in time to hear the good news. So did some other people who had come along on the other side of the gorge. Among them was Cliff Brooks who had returned from Miss Hartfield's house. He waved to his father and asked if anyone was hurt.

"Everyone's alright."

Freddy opened his eyes and groaned in pain.

"You're going to be alright," the sheriff told him.

"I think my leg is broken. It hurts so bad."

The sheriff hollered back to the others, "His leg is broken."

Mr. Gehrmann stepped forward and shouted to the sheriff, "We'll get a board or something to carry him on."

The only thing available was the tailgate of Dave Logan's wagon. Some of the men pulled it off and sent it across the water by rope. The sheriff tied Freddy securely to the tailgate and made sure the leg was held in place.

"How do we get him across?" asked the sheriff.

Mr. Gehrmann shouted his instructions on how they would lift him across. He told the sheriff to tie ropes to the ends of the tailgate, one on each corner.

The sheriff threw the ropes from one end back across the gorge and the other ropes up to Cliff on the road above.

Looking almost like tug-of-war teams, the men raised Freddy and moved him across the gorge to the River Junction side. As he was pulled to safety, everyone let out a big cheer.

Freddy gave a painful smile and said softly, "He heard me, He heard me," and fell asleep again.

Chapter Twenty

In town, at Doctor Powell's office, Mr. Alexander, Mrs. Baxter and Mrs. Malone waited for something to happen. They said later that all they could do was look at one another and hold hands. Without saying a word they told each other how they felt.

When Mr. Baxter rushed into the office he said, "I heard there was an accident. Are you alright?"

Mrs. Baxter began to explain, "I'm fine. It's the boys. The bridge collapsed with Danny and Zach on it. The men went out to find them and bring them back."

"Was Freddy with them?"

"Nobody seems to know," she cried and he put his arm around her.

Miss Polly was watching for the first sign of someone coming into town from the west. She heard the crowd out front beginning to grow louder. Then she noticed a wagon coming from the direction of the depot.

"Here comes a wagon!"

The parents rushed for the door to see who was coming.

We pulled up to Doc Powell's house and climbed out of the wagon. I noticed that my mother was nowhere in sight. I was relieved to know that she had not heard about the accident yet. She would have just worried for no reason.

Mrs. Baxter came running out the door. "Where is he?" She was in a panic, looking all around. "Where's Freddy?"

"Mr. Brooks and Mr. Gehrmann went to get him," I said.

"Get him?" she cried. "Where is he?"

"When the bridge collapsed, he jumped to a ledge and I think he broke his leg. But he sounded OK when I left."

"Oh, honey!" Mrs. Baxter grabbed her husband's arm. "He *is* hurt!"

"Now settle down, Myrtle," said Mr. Baxter. "He's alright."

The crowd started talking again and someone shouted, "Here comes another wagon!"

"It's Mr. Brooks and that stranger!" shouted someone else.

I could overhear the comments of some of the people as the wagon came closer.

"Isn't that the man who's living in the Dobson house?"

"What's he doin' with Andy?"

"It's about time he showed his face in town."

I spoke up. "That's Mr. Gehrmann. He's the one who saved Danny and Zach!"

The wagon came to a stop in front of the house

and Andy jumped down.

"Freddy," said Mrs. Baxter. "Is he with you?"

She looked over the side of the wagon. There was Freddy sound asleep.

"Oh, dear God!" she cried out. "He's dead!"

"No, Mrs. Baxter," said Mr. Brooks, "he's just asleep." But before he could finish saying it, she fainted into her husband's arms.

The Alexanders and the Malones were soon hugging and kissing their sons. Everybody was asking questions about how the boys were.

Mr. Gehrmann stood next to Dave Logan's wagon and just watched what was going on. The people in the crowd were watching the boys and parents. They didn't seem to notice Mr. Gehrmann at all. For the first time in two years he said he felt that he wasn't being looked at like a person in a circus freak show. He smiled and I guessed he was thinking about what he had just done.

Doctor Powell broke up all the hugging and kissing. "I want all you boys to get in my office so I can check you out."

Danny and Zach were relieved and followed him inside as they wiped the kisses from their faces. I waited for a minute.

By that time Freddy was awake and his mother had been revived.

"I prayed, Pa. I prayed that God would help us." Freddy's voice was high-pitched with excitement. "There really is a God, huh, Pa?"

Mr. Baxter smiled and said, "I guess there really is."

Mrs. Baxter hugged her husband and added, "There certainly is."

Andy and Mr. Gehrmann carried Freddy into the house. He was still tied onto the makeshift stretcher. Mr. and Mrs. Baxter walked along beside him. Andy and Mr. Gehrmann put the wooden stretcher and Freddy on one of the cots inside the parlor. Mr. Malone walked over and said to Mr. Gehrmann, "I want to thank you for what you did."

Mr. Alexander added, "And I want to apologize for some of us in River Junction."

"Apologize?" asked Mr. Gehrmann.

"We judged you before we even got a chance to know you," replied Mr. Alexander.

"Thank you, so very much," said Mrs. Baxter with tears in her eyes. "How can we thank you?"

"Seeing you happy is all the thanks I need," answered Mr. Gehrmann. "I just thank God I could be there to help."

"Look at your hands!" exclaimed Miss Polly. His hands were bloody and caked with dirt. "Come in the house and let me clean them up."

Mr. Gehrmann put his big sore hand on my shoulder and said, "Mike here needs some doctoring on his sore hands too." We followed Miss Polly into the house and she and Mrs. Powell started nursing us.

Mr. Gehrmann gasped in pain as Miss Polly poured water over them. She could then see that the skin had been torn away. His hands were a lot worse than mine.

"Oooo, how did this happen?"

"It's a rope burn," he answered.

Mrs. Powell washed off my hands. It hurt but I wasn't going to let on.

The door to the examining room opened. The doctor came out with Danny and Zach. They looked like soldiers returning from the Civil War and I guess they felt almost as bad. "These boys are just fine," he said, "but they're going to be a little sore tomorrow."

"What about Freddy?" asked Mr. Baxter.

"I'm going to set his leg and put it in a cast. He'll be in a lot of pain for a while, but in a few months he'll be back to normal."

Mrs. Powell finished bandaging my hands and went into the examining room to help her husband with Freddy.

Mr. Gehrmann let out a big groan as Miss Polly put some medicine on his hands. Without thinking about what she was saying, she blurted out, "I hope this doesn't leave a scar."

The room was as silent as could be as everyone realized what she had said. Then *she* realized what she had said and looked up at Mr. Gehrmann's badly scarred face. Before she could say she was sorry, Mr. Gehrmann broke into laughter.

Miss Polly laughed, too.

Then we all joined in.

Chapter Twenty-one

Even though the door was closed to the examining room we could hear Freddy cry out in pain as the doctor pulled his fractured leg bone into place. Without anybody saying it, everyone felt uneasy about being able to hear Freddy. Mrs. Powell came out and said, "I think we should leave the Baxters and Freddy alone with Doc."

Everyone walked out onto the porch. By then the crowd had broken up and the town was nearly back to normal. As they walked past Mr. Gehrmann, Danny and Zach thanked him again.

"I sure liked the way you handled that rope, Mr. Gehrmann," said Zach. He looked as though he might be wondering if Mr. Gehrmann was going to say something. Danny was also nervous about what Mr. Gehrmann might say.

"Maybe some day *you'll* learn how to handle a rope," said Mr. Gehrmann. He smiled at the boys. I guess their parents never knew what their sons had done to Mr. Gehrmann. But Mr. Gehrmann always used every chance he had to tease the boys about it.

"Can we take you home, Mike?" asked Mr. Malone.

"I'll take him home," said Mr. Gehrmann. "My wagon is right over here."

The parents and friends thanked him. He said, "I'm glad I was there to help." He was buried under the hugs and kisses of the mothers. The fathers patted him on the back. He seemed pleased by all the attention, but he looked awkward in accepting it.

Mr. Gehrmann and I climbed into his wagon. He and I were a funny sight with our hands wrapped in those snow-white bandages. As we rolled slowly along the main street in the wagon, the few people still on the street waved and hollered to Mr. Gehrmann.

"Good job, Mr. Gehrmann!"

"Hello, Mike. Hello, Mr. Gehrmann!"

"I think I'm going to like it around here, Mike. In fact, I was just thinking about opening up a clock shop. Do you think anybody would want to buy clocks or have them fixed?"

"I know my mother would."

He pulled the wagon to a stop as he looked around the town. It was as though he was picking out a place for his new shop.

I didn't know whether or not to ask because I thought he might think I was too young and inexperienced, but I asked anyhow, "Will you need any help?"

"Sure, would you like to work for me?"

"Yeah!"

"We can talk it over with your parents."

"No," I said, "please don't talk to them yet." I explained how they felt about me working.

"Well, we'll see," he said. "Where do you live, Mike?"

"Just up the road on the right."

He ordered Samson to move along and the wagon began rolling slowly toward our house.

"You've got quite a story to tell your folks," he said. "Would you like for me to come in with you?"

"Sure, that might help."

Before the wagon came to a complete stop, Mother was out on the porch. "Mike, what are you doing home?" She ran toward the wagon. As she came closer, she could see our messy clothes and our bandaged hands.

"What happened to you two? Michael, your hands!"

"It's a long story, Mother, but we're fine. Don't worry about us."

"You must be Mr. Gehrmann."

"Yes, I'm pleased to meet you, Mrs. Roberts."

"Mike has told me a lot about you. Please come in."

She looked us up and down and said, "It looks like you two have an interesting story to tell."

As we sat in the kitchen telling the story, I could see that Mother was unhappy about something and I knew what it was.

"Michael, you disobeyed me, didn't you?"

"Yes."

"Michael Roberts, I'm upset with you for disobeying me, but I guess it was meant to be that you were there to help."

I smiled.

She didn't.

"If you would agree, Mr. Gehrmann, maybe Michael can work off his punishment by helping you around your house."

Mr. Gehrmann hesitated as though he was making a very important decision. "You know, I've been thinking of opening up a clock shop in town. He could help me get that set up."

"That sounds fine," said Mother.

"But I would have to pay him for some of the work he does—" Mr. Gehrmann began.

My mother interrupted, "Oh, that won't be necessary, Mr. Gehrmann."

"Oh, but I think I should," he said. "Does that sound fair, Mike?"

I tried to act as though I didn't care one way or the other and answered, "I guess so."

"Then it's settled." Mr. Gehrmann turned his head so Mother couldn't see his face and gave me a wink. I succeeded in keeping my big smile from showing on my face.

"Now you go on outside, Mike. Mr. Gehrmann and I need to get acquainted."

I thought I would use the chance to finish some of the work on the sewing machine. I went out to the barn and latched the door behind me.

There is something distinct about the inside of an old barn. The smells of animals, hay, and dust mix together in a unique way. On that day, the smell was not nearly as dusty. The dampness of the storm still hung in the air and the barn smelled like a freshly plowed field.

I opened the tool chest lid. It banged against the side wall of the barn. There was something missing. Two hunting rifles, my dad's favorites, were missing.

As I picked up the tools I realized I couldn't do

anything with bandaged hands. I kept thinking about those guns. Dad had no reason to take them with him that day. I wondered if someone could have stolen them.

"Michael!" Mother was calling. "Are you out there?"

I dropped the tools back into the chest and slammed the lid down.

"I'm coming."

Chapter Twenty-two

I ran out of the barn and closed the door behind me. Mother was standing in the doorway on the back porch. I was afraid she was going to call me in for one of those talks.

"I think we'd better have a talk, Michael. Come in here."

She called me Michael again. That was a bad sign. I took my time getting into the house, but a person can only walk so slowly without looking a little crazy.

"Michael, what are we going to do with you?"

That's one of those questions that parents ask. They know you can't answer it and they don't expect you to. I just shrugged my shoulders and stared at my feet.

"Look at me when I'm talking to you." That's another favorite thing for parents to say when they're having a one-sided discussion with you. I wondered if they thought I could really hear better if I looked at them.

When I looked up, Mother stopped what she was saying and looked me straight in the eyes. She didn't say anything for what seemed like five minutes. Then she grabbed me and gave me a great big hug and a kiss. I just hoped she wasn't going to cry and drip tears down my neck.

While still hugging me tight, she said, "Let's not talk about this anymore. I'm just so thankful you're alright."

I knew it would happen. A warm teardrop rolled down my neck and under my collar.

The front door swung open and startled us. It was Dad. "Are you alright, Mike?" I was getting hugged again.

"Sure, Dad, but how did you get back over the gorge with the bridge out?"

"When Cliff came to tell us about the accident, I decided to hurry home and make sure you were alright. I rode Bessie up to the railroad trestle bridge. I walked her across there and we rode home."

Dad looked over at Mother and asked, "Are *you* alright?"

"Yes, I'm fine," she sighed. "I didn't know a thing about the accident until Mike was safely home."

"Mike, you were disobeying instructions, weren't you?" Dad asked.

Mother spoke up, "We've already talked about that."

"Well, maybe Mike and I should have a talk out in the barn." I thought Mother was thinking that Dad had a spanking in mind. Dad winked at me and we both knew what we were going to do.

"Come on, Mike."

"Dinner will be ready in about half an hour," said Mother with a look on her face that told Dad, "Be gentle."

I didn't know if Dad was going to lecture me on the things that had happened. I decided to change the subject before it came up. As Dad pulled open the barn door, I asked, "Dad, did you know your guns are missing?"

"Yes."

"What happened to them?"

"I sold them."

"Sold them! Why?"

"Because I didn't have enough money to buy the sewing machine."

"But you said I could have one of those guns some day. Remember?"

"Aren't you being a little selfish? Just remember that we're doing this for your mother."

I didn't answer him because I was disappointed to think I wouldn't be able to get the gun I had always looked forward to having.

"Don't worry," he said. "Mr. Strump promised to keep the guns until I can afford to buy them back."

We didn't say anything more about the guns. Dad and I climbed up into the loft. He worked on the sewing machine while I handed him the tools. Dad lowered it carefully to the dirt floor of the barn and we covered it with a tarp, stood there catching our breath, and smiled with pride in what we had done.

"You run in and see if you can keep your mother's attention away from the back door until I can get this thing inside."

"OK, Dad." I ran across the yard and onto the

porch. I picked up some wood with my bandaged hands and carried it inside to the kitchen.

"Need more wood?" I asked.

"Yes, thanks, Mike," said Mother. "Be careful. You'll hurt your hands."

My hands felt a little better by then, but that gave me an idea. As I put down the wood I cried out, "Ow!"

"Oh, let me see what you did, Mike." She unwrapped the bandage to see how my hands were.

Over her shoulder I could see my big, strong dad carrying that bulky machine through the doorway. He was trying to keep from grunting out loud.

Thud! The machine dropped the last few inches as his grip gave way.

Mother turned to see what the noise was. "What on earth are you bringing into this house?"

Dad lifted off the tarp and there stood the surprise. She didn't say a word at first. She walked slowly over to it and looked it over as though she was deciding if she wanted to buy it.

"Happy anniversary!"

"But we can't afford this," she told Dad.

"It's already paid for," said Dad.

"Oh, thank you!" She threw her arms around Dad's neck and gave him a big kiss.

"You can thank Mike too." He made a big fake smile behind Mother's back to tell me that he wanted me to smile too. I smiled as Mother came over and gave me a big hug. I was smiling on the outside, but inside I was wondering if I would ever get my gun.

Mother put a chair in front of the sewing machine. She ran her hands over it as if it were a soft kitten. She put her feet on the foot pedal and began rocking it back and forth. The machine clanked into action and the needle moved up and down.

Dinner was late that night—Dad and I fixed it.

Chapter Twenty-three

The fire was beginning to die down and it was getting late. Dad and I were playing our eighth game of checkers and Mother was still sewing away on her new machine. Checkers was becoming more difficult for me to win. I'm sure Dad let me win when I was younger. But as I got older, the games got more and more competitive. Sometimes we would even bet a couple of chores on the outcome of the game. Dad always played much better when he didn't want to feed the chickens or gather the firewood.

We were startled by a knock at the door.

Mother stopped pedaling, turned her head toward the door and said, "Who could that be at this time of night?" That's another one of those questions that doesn't need or get an answer.

Dad went to the door and opened it. There stood Mr. Strump with his hat in his hands and a big grin on his plump face.

"Evenin'," he said. "I hope I didn't come too late."

"No, of course not," said Dad. "Come on in." Have you ever noticed how people will say no when they are really thinking yes?

"Good evening," Mr. Strump nodded to Mother.

"Good evening. May I get you a cup of coffee?"

"No, thanks," he said. "I can't stay long. I'm going around telling everyone about the meeting we had at the depot tonight."

"About what?" asked Dad.

"Well, we talked about getting the bridge rebuilt. We need to do it soon."

Mother spoke up, "Yes, or we'll have to miss church this Sunday and the children will have to miss school." River Junction lost its church building in the fire of 1883 along with many other buildings in the south part of town. The only other big building in the area was our schoolhouse clear over in Pine Ridge. In 1898 it was still being used as a church building on Sundays.

"We decided to have a 'bridge raising' this Thursday," he said.

"Sounds like a great idea," said Dad. "What can *I* do?"

"Well, we were thinking maybe you and Mr. Foster could be in charge of getting the timbers cut and delivered."

"Sure, but we'll need some more men to help get that much wood ready by Thursday."

"That won't be a problem. We're all getting together at sunrise tomorrow at the depot. Then we can decide which job each person will do. Tomorrow we get everything together and Thursday morning we'll be ready to raise a new bridge."

Mr. Strump seemed to take great pride in being the organizer of the project.

"That sounds great," said Dad. "I'll be there."

"If we're going to raise a bridge we'll need to have lots of food ready for the workers," said Mother. "Who's in charge of the food?"

"Miss Polly is in charge and wants to meet with all the women at the courthouse tomorrow at noon."

Mother said, "It sounds great. We haven't raised a building around here in years."

"Well, I gotta go," said Mr. Strump. "I know he won't be able to do much work with those sore hands of his but I thought it would be nice to give Mr. Gehrmann a personal invitation, so I'm going out there to see him tomorrow."

"I'm sure he'll appreciate that," said Mother.

Mr. Strump stepped out the door and we said our good-byes. Dad closed the door and slid the latch into place. He pulled out his pocket watch and snapped open the cover. "Well, I guess we better be getting to bed. It's going to be a long day tomorrow."

Chapter Twenty-four

The scene of Tuesday's accident began to take on a carnival look by early Thursday morning. Makeshift tables were set up in the grassy meadow overlooking the gorge. They were covered with brightly colored tablecloths and stacked with baskets of food and drinks. The women of the town, under the direction of Miss Polly, gathered together a fantastic menu: fried chicken, potato salad, corn on the cob, homemade pickles, biscuits, honey, butter, and many delicious desserts.

Wagonloads of people headed out of River Junction along Creek Road and left the town nearly deserted. As more and more people arrived at the edge of the gorge, a crowd gathered and stared in amazement at the remains of the old bridge. The men soon became involved in a discussion about how to build a new bridge. There were no plans or diagrams to follow until a few were drawn in the dirt with sticks. The drawings were discussed, rubbed out by heavy boots, and redrawn until everyone agreed on the final design.

The Baxters arrived in their wagon with Freddy riding in back. His leg was in a huge cast and propped on a big grain sack to cushion it. Mr. Baxter pulled the wagon up near the edge of the gorge so that Freddy could sit and watch the bridge being built. Danny and Zach soon arrived and we all sat with Freddy to watch.

It wasn't long before the first new pilings were secured into place and the bridge began to grow. The activity reminded me of the times I had watched colonies of ants busily going about their work.

We were so involved with watching the work that we didn't notice Mr. Gehrmann's wagon coming down the road. He walked up behind us and in his deep voice startled us as he said, "Have you boys seen a bridge around here?"

We all laughed and Danny pointed downstream and said, "It went thataway."

Mr. Gehrmann shouted to Mr. Strump, "What can I do to help?"

"Give your hands a rest, Mr. Gehrmann. We've got plenty of manpower. But you could gather some more ropes together. We'll need them to lower the big timbers into place."

Mr. Gehrmann grinned at Danny and Zach. "Could you boys get some ropes from my wagon?"

"Sure," they answered. They were wondering what he would say next.

His grin grew bigger and bigger and he said, "Don't forget that long one. You know which one I mean?"

They nodded and grinned at each other. They

would never forget that particular rope.

The men worked in shifts right on through the day. They stopped to grab a few bites to eat at lunchtime and rushed back to work. We wanted to get in on the work but our parents seemed to think we would just get in the way.

Mr Gehrmann said, "I've got an idea." He went over to talk with Mr. Strump. Mr. Strump pointed to one of the large timbers lying near the edge of the gorge. "That one," he said. We wondered what Mr. Gehrmann had in mind.

"Come on, boys and girls," he said, "and help me carry this thing under that tree."

"What are we going to do, Mr. Gehrmann?" asked Zach.

"You'll see."

There were so many of us that the huge timber didn't seem heavy at all. We soon had it under the big oak tree and out of the direct sun which had grown quite warm.

Mr. Gehrmann went to his wagon and returned with some tools. He began making marks on the wood. All of us stood silently watching and wondering. We strained to see what the marks were. In big block letters and numbers he scratched into the beam: BUILT IN 1898.

"OK," he said. "Let's start carving!"

The great part of the afternoon was spent sitting under that old tree and carving the letters and numbers deep into the beam. Mr. Gehrmann sat with us and we talked about many things. He told us stories of San Francisco as he carved a fancy border for our sign. We were so interested in his stories that we didn't notice that Danny had sneaked down to the other end of the beam. He sat there carving his name into the wood. When we finally noticed what he was doing, we joined in. At one end of the beam was a beautiful sign and at the other were the names of most of the children in River Junction.

"We're ready for that section of the bridge, Mr. Gehrmann!" called Mr. Strump.

"OK, boys and girls," said Mr. Gehrmann, "move it into place."

The roadbed of the bridge was finished and we were the first to walk across it. We proudly carried the huge timber clear across the big bridge and all the way back. The adults stood and watched. When we got back to the River Junction side, we put the beam into place and they clapped and cheered.

The men were soon back to work and we watched as the final boards were bolted into place and the railings attached to the sides.

The sun dropped below the trees and there stood a new, sturdy bridge in the golden glow of the sunset. The pounding noises that had gone on almost without stopping since morning finally stopped. The only sounds were those of the wind blowing through the trees and the water rushing over the rocks.

"It's time to eat!" shouted Miss Polly. Everyone whooped and hollered as we rushed toward the tables. Before the dust could even settle, there was the familiar sound of silverware clanking against plates. But the noise of dozens of conversations soon filled the air. Occasionally someone would stand and offer a toast.

"To the new bridge."

"May it serve us well."

Everyone would echo the toasts and then return to eating and talking. Mr. Malone brought out his fiddle and began squeaking out a tune. A few harmonicas joined in. Anyone with a free pair of hands began clapping along.

The song was finished and Mr. Baxter stood to give another toast. He called for everyone's attention. The sounds of conversation and eating hushed, and he spoke, "I would like to make a toast." He raised his glass toward Mr. Gehrmann. Before he could say anything more, there came shouts, "To Mr. Gehrmann!"

Mr. Gehrmann stood and raised his hands as a sign to stop. Again the noise faded. Mr. Baxter patted him on the back and said, "We're sorry we didn't make you feel welcome at first. But now we would all like to welcome you officially to River Junction." He raised his glass and took a drink. Many voices joined in, "Welcome, Mr. Gehrmann!" There was an unusual silence as everyone waited for Mr. Gehrmann to speak.

He seemed to be thinking about what to say. He coughed into his bandaged hand and cleared his throat. "I— I— really don't know how to say this," he began. "You people are the ones who should be receiving *my* thanks."

We glanced at one another, silently asking what he meant.

He continued. "I realize now how close the people of a small town can be and how you might be somewhat afraid of a stranger, especially when he hasn't told you everything about himself."

He hesitated. "I have more to tell you.

"It happened over two years ago. I had been working late and was walking home. We lived on a hill in San Francisco. I started walking up the hill from the downtown area and I noticed a fire burning on the hill. As I got closer, I could see that it was our house. I ran up that hill as fast as I could. By the time I got there, the fire had spread through most of the house."

He stopped, pressed his lips together, and swallowed.

He continued. "My parents, my wife and our daughter were all asleep when the fire started. I ran into the house and up the stairway. I got about halfway up when it collapsed. I fell into the fire below. Someone pulled me from the flames and covered me to put out the fire. The fire wagon arrived, but it was too late."

He stopped, swallowed, and blinked his watery eyes.

Then he said slowly, with a crack in his voice, "My whole family died that night."

A tear rolled down his scarred cheek. I had never seen a man cry before. A painful lump formed in my throat. I tried to hold back my tears. I couldn't.

Mr. Gehrmann wiped his eyes and cleared his throat again.

"When my accident happened and I lost my family, I just couldn't understand why it had happened to *me*. If *I* couldn't understand it, then there was no way to explain it to others. For that reason, I gave up the most important thing in my life— being a minister."

There were gasps of surprise. The large crowd erupted into conversation. Mr. Gehrmann spoke loudly to be heard. "But— but things that have happened here the last few days have made me feel that there is a reason for me being here. I would like to stay if you want me. I think I'm ready to return to my work."

There were shouts of approval and people gathered around to tell him how they felt. A big smile grew on his disfigured face. Firm pats on the back nearly knocked him over.

Mr. Strump waved his hands and shouted to get the attention of everyone. The noise began to die down. He stood up on the bench of a nearby table to say, "If everyone feels up to it, I think we should have a 'church raising' just as soon as possible."

The people of River Junction broke into cheers and applause as they gathered closer to Mr. Gehrmann.

Chapter Twenty-Five

More lanterns were lit as the darkness settled over the meadow. Mr. Gehrmann was surely enjoying himself as he moved from table to table to talk to everyone.

He joined us at our table and the discussion began.

"Do you miss San Francisco?" Mother asked.

"Yes," he said. "I had many good times there."

"My father loved that city," Mother said.

"What was his name?" Mr. Gehrmann asked as though he was already fairly sure of the answer.

"John Haley," said Mother. "John David Haley, but everybody called him—"

"J.D.," interrupted Mr. Gehrmann.

"Yes, you *knew* him!"

Mr. Gehrmann hesitated. It was as though he wanted to speak, but couldn't. His eyes became watery, reflecting the glistening light from the lanterns around us. He nodded to Mother but still said nothing.

Finally the words came, "I met him a short time before the accident. He had just moved into our neighborhood."

"I remember when he moved," Mother spoke up. "That was just before he—he had his heart attack."

A tear rolled down Mr. Gehrmann's scarred cheek as he hesitated again. "He was there that night, the night of the fire. He was the one who pulled me out."

Mother smiled. "He saved your life?!"

He nodded in agreement. His long pause told Mother the rest of the story before he could begin to tell it. "He was burned so badly."

Then Mother's eyes were full of tears. Dad hugged her tightly.

Mr. Gehrmann continued. "He didn't want anyone to know how bad he was. He didn't want to be seen. He was so badly burned."

Dad spoke up. "But we were told that he died suddenly of a heart attack."

"He didn't want you to worry so he asked the doctor to tell you that. He wanted to be remembered the way he was."

Mother began to cry and wrapped her arms around Mr. Gehrmann. He hugged her too.

"Thank you," said Mother.

"I knew you would want to know."

Mother and Dad nodded and smiled.

The sound of fiddle music echoed through the gorge. The dancing and eating and singing continued late into the evening. Mother and Mr. Gehrmann spent hours sharing the stories about

Grandpa. We knew then that Grandpa's stories about River Junction had led Mr. Gehrmann to us. Grandpa must have known that Mr. Gehrmann would learn to love River Junction as *he* had. In the months and years to follow, a part of Grandpa lived again in River Junction.

Postscript

By Christmas of that year there was a new church standing in the meadow by the bridge, right between River Junction and Pine Ridge. Its tall, white steeple rose high above the old gnarled oak trees. The Reverend Gehrmann, who insisted we still call him Mr. Gehrmann, stood at the top of the steps every Sunday and greeted people as they entered. He was never afraid to show his scarred face or reach out his disfigured hand for a firm, friendly handshake.

The clock shop was also open and going strong with me as the shopkeeper. I was able to save most of the money I needed for Christmas. Most of my money and some of Mother's was spent on Dad's surprise Christmas gift. I bought back his guns from Mr. Strump. Dad never expected such a gift. The rest of the money was spent on a beautiful, chiming mantel clock for Mother.

The New Year, 1899, brought hopes of a better life. The crops grew well in the plentiful rains, the Spanish-American War had come to an end, Freddy was running around on two strong legs, and Louisa Foster agreed to go with me to the spring square dance.

The turn of the century brought a few changes to River Junction; life was fairly calm and undisturbed. The biggest change came when Miss Polly became Mrs. Gehrmann. That was perhaps the greatest change Mr. Gehrmann brought to River Junction—he changed the town gossip into a minister's wife.

I took up working at the newspaper with Emily Collins and spent my free time writing books. Well, some of my free time was spent with Louisa Foster. She became Mrs. Michael Roberts in 1911. The wedding took place in the big, white church next to the bridge. And, of course, Mr. Gehrmann did the ceremony. Our twins were born in 1913.

Danny, of all people, became the sheriff. I guess he knew more about trouble than anyone. He was usually in it or around it as a boy. As a reminder of his childhood, there was a coiled rope hanging on the wall over his desk. Many people thought of it as the rope that was used to rescue him. But there were some of us who knew the real reason Mr. Gehrmann had given it to him.

Freddy and Zach left River Junction. Zach went back East to play professional baseball. He never made the majors and we lost track of him.

Freddy went off to college and seminary. He always hoped to work with Mr. Gehrmann and maybe someday be the minister of our church. His dreams came true.

The 1920s brought prosperity to River Junction but the Great Depression of the 1930s brought many hardships. And Mr. Gehrmann was always there to help. If you couldn't find him at the church, he was at his clock shop.

Mr. Gehrmann became a close friend to all of us. Our acceptance of him restored his faith. And his strength through all the hard times inspired us. He seemed to make the happy times happier and the sad times more bearable. We learned to trust God for the most important things in life. Caring for other people became our number-one concern and from then on all strangers were welcome to River Junction

Almost as suddenly as he had come to River Junction, Mr. Gehrmann left us in 1939. As he sat in a meeting at the depot, a heart attack took his life. It was a great loss to the people of our town. Everyone agreed when *Mayor* Alexander officially renamed River Junction. From that day on, our town was known as "Gehrmannville."

That little house on the outskirts of town has never been lived in since Polly joined her husband in 1945. The trees, bushes, and weeds nearly hide it from sight. And all the windows have been broken out by generation after generation of rock-throwing boys.

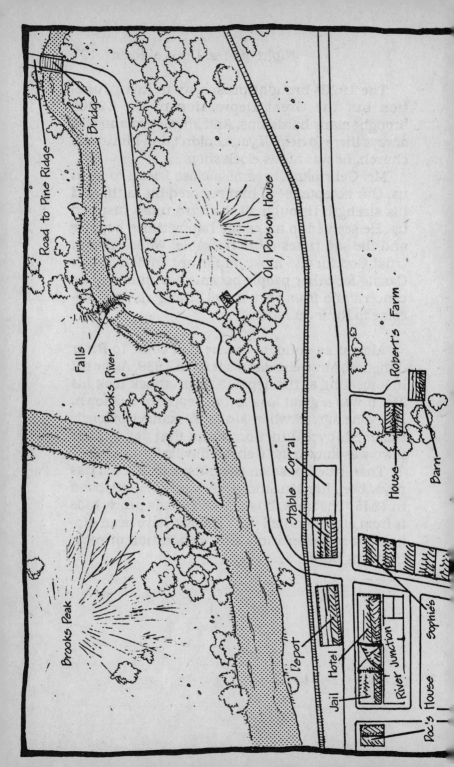